Apocalypse Virus: Initial Infection
Book 1

By: Kirtland D. Neal

To my brothers, thank you for always supporting me and pushing me to be better than I am.

Other Titles by this Author

-Apocalypse Virus: Symptomatic
-Apocalypse Virus: Deterioration
-Apocalypse Virus: Inoperable
-Apocalypse Virus: System Failure
-Inner Workings: Poetic Therapy
-Inner Workings: The Relapse

Chapter 1

Tampa, Florida

January 2nd, 2030

Dillon Thompson wakes up to a devastated apartment that looks as though it had been the scene of a burglary followed by a tornado. For a moment he has no idea why the hell he feels as bad as he does or what happened to his apartment. He lays there a while longer as bits and pieces of memories come meandering back to him. As he raises his large frame up from the floor the pounding in his head tells him to just go back to sleep. And he so desperately wants to listen. Unfortunately for him and his body that whole being an adult thing can be a real bitch sometimes. Every ounce of his being aches as his arms deafly begin to drag themselves from their resting place against his sides to be planted beneath his shoulders. He is besieged by a thunderous and excruciating beating, as though his head was filling in for drummer of a rock band, and that band is currently playing a punk rock banger. Unfortunately, he doesn't have the luxury or ability to ignore the already lengthy mental list of things he needs to do today. So, fighting the fits of nausea, he staggers his way up to his lumbering height of six foot five inches, taking a moment to allow the room to settle from its spinning performance.

Kirtland D. Neal

Once he is sure he isn't going to puke from dizziness he surveys the damage left in the wake of the last three days. The glass coffee table is shattered into countless glistening pieces. Again. Luckily there doesn't appear to be any blood around the fragmented coffee table this time. The balcony windows are either covered in smudges from unidentifiable body parts, he does not want to know which ones in particular had been pressed against his windows; or covered with streaks of alcohol and vomit. Yet however besmirched and contaminated, still they permitted the blinding amber light of the mid-morning sun to penetrate the disaster area causing his head to pound growingly harder making it hard for him to focus his thoughts. It isn't the worse his head had ever throbbed, but it is damn sure close. The fridge is cast ajar with the luminescent bulb flickering in with an epileptic rhythm, whatever food was inside is no doubt spoiled by this point.

The apartment is filled with countless bodies. Hopefully, all living, but he would have to check. The smell is funky enough that someone could very well be dead, and no one noticed until now. There is such a fierce aroma of booze, vomit, shit, and piss that it is nauseating. It is more packed than any mosh pit he had ever been in. It seems that all the spaces where a person isn't passed out are stacked with bottles, clothes, solo cups, kegs, and other garbage. A small part of him is borderline impressed and proud at the sheer number of people he had packed into this place as well as the grand scale of the party. The couch is covered in unsavory bodily fluids, much like most of the floor. Both of which would probably have to be replaced now. There is no telling how amazing it will look from the numerous cameras he had placed around the residency with the foresight that he would likely black out. He blacked out just after the dropping of the ball. He still had clothes on at that point. Now he stands in the middle of the room, as naked as a newborn. Looking over everything and everyone left in the wake of this New Year's Eve party. If this cluster fuck of a room is to be of any hint as to the scope of the festivities, then it was above par for the course as far as he was concerned. This party may very well have been the best he has ever had the pleasure of throwing in his almost four decades of life.

"Well fuuuck." He groans under his breath as he runs his hands over his stubbly face. He pauses for a moment to marvel at the length of the stubble, a clear indication that this party had lasted way longer than he ever expected. He would have to check what day it was after finding where his phone wondered off to.

Having finished checking out the aftermath, he searched for his clothes while others tossed and turned as he rummaged through the room. At one point he gets knocked over when someone rolls over where he was about to step. This warrants a chorus of groans and profanity to rise from the disgruntled sleeping degenerates he calls friends. He almost doesn't get up after he falls, however he finds the urge to relieve himself too strong to simply lay there any longer. He staggers his way to the very much occupied master bathroom to take a piss while trying to pretend that there isn't a naked couple interlocked with each other in his bathtub still. It looked as though they had both fallen asleep during sex. Dillon found it equal parts interesting and concerning. The sight brought a simple grin to his face. He resumed his search and recovery mission for his clothes after the bathroom side show.

The search effort proves fruitless when fifteen minutes later a frustrated and hungover Dillon goes into what was formerly known as his room. He grabs the first lazy outfit he can assemble. Some bleach splattered blue jeans and a tattered vintage rock tank top are the lucky winners. He was proud of the hand cut job he had done on the old shirt a few years ago. He spends a great deal of time in search of his phone once he is finished getting dressed. He needs tuneage for what he was about to do. For what he must do next.

"What the fuck!?" Dillon blurts out as he sees what time it is for the first time. He is quickly yelled at to shut the fuck up by the semiconscious party goers. According to his phone it is 0800 on January 2nd. This party had started at 1800 on December 31st. Some of the guest would undoubtable be in trouble with spouses and bosses. Or both if they were that unfortunate.

He already knew what the first song would be before he even hooked the aux cord up. He turned the volume all the way up right as the song began. *Boom-boom clap. Boom-boom clap. 'Buddy you're a big boy....'* And just like that Queen was dominating the airwaves of the high-rise apartment. He feels the vibrations from the speakers in his bones. The music is so loud it causes most everyone else to get up and leave after saying goodbye within the first three or four songs.

After about thirty minutes of Dillon's clean up only four people remain. Michael Mathews, one of Dillon's best friends from high school. Although he was a bit more country than Dillon their friendship seemed almost perfect, like how you wouldn't expect two vastly different things to go together yet somehow the pairing seemed to compliment both. Just like Chicken nuggets dipped in chocolate pudding. Mike is scrubbing all the residues out of the couch while he has one of Dillon's shirts covering his face. It is unclear what some of them might have been. However, it is rather obvious that the gloves he wore were well warranted. Mikey had gotten married and had a baby not long after all of them had graduated high school. Between that baby and a pregnant wife, he had been given plenty of practice at scrubbing bodily fluids out of things. The smell still bothered him, a statement his face seemed to easily make.

He needed this trip not only as a break from his job at the factory but also as a break from his wife, and their children. Not to say that Dillon didn't love his nephews or Asher who was like a sister to him, but he also knew that Mikey was the best husband and father he could be. A much better one than Dillon could have been in the same situation. That translates to total exhaustion and no time or money for himself. (So, for all of y'all with an awesome parent or spouse make sure you show them some gratitude and take care of them.)

Lucas Jay, Dillon's oldest friend who was the only one from their group of friends at school to have also served in the military besides Dillon. Luke is in the process of trying get one of those bras with the metal underwire unstuck from the garbage disposal. No one had any idea who's bra it was. And there were even less ideas as to how it got there. Someone did find a video later though, and well…. Well yeah, the video just raised more questions than it answers. On the flip side they did get to see the pair of boobs that were once in the bra. Needless to say, she would definitely be invited back to every party in the future. Or maybe Dillon would just invite her over for a little one on one ropes course.

Paul Bishop, or PB as everyone called him, was the one friend in the group who was great around the bros but never had any luck with the women. He is currently trying to clean up the kitchen. Emphasis on the trying. Not a whole lot of succeeding on that front. What is it they say at the end of those infomercials, results may vary or something like that? There is what looks like a puddle of melted ice cream and water flowing out of the freezer which seems to merge with spilled post party cocktail that stained or covered most of the apartment. Yep, Dillon was absolutely going to need to replace flooring for the entire residency within the next week or so.

Then, there was Ricci Lemons, Dillon's old roommate. Ricci is still passed out cuddling with a lamp shade next to the TV. Not the first time he has cuddled with a lamp shade, probably not the last either. Yup, he is that friend. Thankfully, the music was too loud for anyone else besides Dillon to hear what he was telling Mrs. Kennedy he would do to her. It's simply better no one thinks about why he is so in love with her. Dillon had learned to leave that one alone not soon after they met. It sends a cold, disturbing shiver down his back when he hears his friend talk like that. The kind of shiver that makes you skin and muscles crawl all over your body. That answer raised more questions than it resolved. So, Dillon had gotten into the habit of tuning his friend out at times like this, more for Dillon's own sanity than anything else.   And it takes a lot to make the big man feel uneasy when talking about sexcapades.

A few hours later they take a break to go grab some food. While the apartment is starting to look like its former self it is still in no condition for them to be eating in it just yet. Also, all the food had either gone bad when the fridge and freezer were left open or it had been eaten over the three day long party. So, after opening up all the windows to air out the apartment they found themselves heading towards a little whole in the wall place down the street, Stinky Pete's.

Damn it was hot. Dillon thinks to himself as he feels the first few beads of sweat begin to form. Funny thing about south and central Florida was that it be 85 degrees on Christmas and then back up into the 90's by New Year's. They always had lunch at the bar anytime one of them came to visit Dillon. Now Stinky Pete's was not as bad as it might sound. It was about a twenty-minute walk from Dillon's apartment building.

Stinky Pete's lies in the old rust-red colored brick building at the corner of East 12th Avenue and North 21st Street right next to I-4. A beautiful piece of property that in a distant past might have been one of the numerous old cigar factories that had littered Ybor City over a century ago. The perfume of rich tobacco had soaked up in the brick work from the countless years of operation. It had been renovated of course. The second and third floor had been redone for Thaddeus Castello, the owner, too live with his wife and young daughter. It was by no means lacking in rooms or space, allowing the family to be extremely comfortable. He had named the bar after his old man who had passed away a few weeks before Thad finished renovations. The bar and kitchen took up about a third of the downstairs. The middle third if you were looking at it from either 11th or 12th Avenue.

The bar was in the shape of a horseshoe and the bar top was made of wood that Thad and his dad had found on a scuba trip through the ship wreck speckled shorelines many miles off the shores of the Florida Keys. They got some of their diving friends to help recover the massive weathered board and dropped a pretty penny to ship it back to Tampa. Now stained, the smooth old wood was a deep warm brown and laid upon old scuba tanks which had been emptied and had the tops removed and were welded together with a metal pole fixed just inches off the ground that served as a foot rest for the bar patrons. The bar had writing carved and scribbled across the top. Thad liked it, said it made it everyone's place, which is what he wanted most from this bar. It was meant to be somewhere everyone would feel included and like family. The bar stools were all different, stools that Thad had found through various garage sales, dump adventures and some were even made by Thad himself. Some people have even brought in stools and chairs to either give to the bar or trade for another chair or a few free drinks. There was a new chair in there at least once a month it seemed like. The bar was stockpiled with so many different types of liquor that you lost count before you changed from counting vodkas to rums or anything else, yet it always had what you wanted and no bottle stayed full for more than a few days.

The floor was the same as it had been back when the building was first built, only now the old stone floor was painted with a mural of the old shipwrecks that Thad and old Pete loved so much. An assortment of sea life surrounded the ghost ships. There are a few pieces missing from a bar fight or two. One may or may not have been Dillon's fault, but who's to say. It wasn't his fault that big guy's wife didn't have her ring on.

The booths and tables, much like the bar stools were all unique. One of the tables was actually once a nice old table that some family used to eat around on the holidays, but now it's once lavishly carved legs had been replaced with sturdy and rugged wooden legs. They were only replaced after Dillon slammed a man through it one night and the legs broke. Once again, he would argue that he didn't start that fight. The walls of the bar resembled the bar top with signatures, various writings and pictures sketched along them plus the countless pictures people had pinned up and some street art that was hung there as well. Thad even had pictures drawn by some of the neighborhood kids. He was undoubtable the most caring and gruff person that Dillon had ever known.

Through a set of old saloons looking doors behind the bar was the kitchen, which he added on to the back of the bar reaching out towards 11th Avenue It was not incredibly big, but it was perfect for this quaint bar. There was a fully stocked ten feet deep walk-in pantry, a sister walk-in fridge as well as a walk-in freezer. Each just as deep and well stocked as the last. Two twin deep fryers. An industrial dishwasher. Two sandwich presses for Cubans. And a glorious top of the line, ten burner stove and six by four-foot grill. A counter extended several feet out on both sides of the grill and stove for prep work. This feature acted as an island in the kitchen. There was an ice machine built into the wall between the bar and kitchen so it could be accessed from both sides. The front door opened just twenty feet from the mouth of the horseshoe bar. One of those old heavy metal doors like you might find in an old dungeon or something. There was the archway that had been used for Thad and Jill's wedding ceremony. It was now covered with various clothes and other memories people had tied up over and a halo of Christmas lights that never got taken down.

From there, doors were set against the walls to either side of the kitchen. The black and red speckled metal door all the way against the far back right hand side led into an exterior enclosed stairwell that ascended to Thad's living quarters. There was second door put in catty corner just a few feet down the right-hand wall. The bluish-grey metal door led to the massive garage Thad made during the renovations. The biggest obstacle of converting that side to a garage was knocking down one of the walls to install the massive garage doors without destroying that side of the upstairs. He made sure this cave of his was stocked with all the best tools he could find. He preferred to do any repairs himself. There was a stockpile of chairs people left that were to be used when one was broken inside. He even had one of the car lifts like professional auto shops have which allowed him to work on his cars if he needed to bring it in here.

The door far to the left of the bar and kitchen led to a large corridor with countless doors. The hallway walls were cover with cheap wallpaper and adorned with all sorts of pictures and letters that people had thumbtacked on it over the years. There was plenty of sharpie graffiti left by kids and drunks alike. Behind each door was a bed, a toilet, a sink and a barf bucket.

Dillon had been a coming there for almost a year before he figured out firsthand why Thad had the rooms back there. Thad had put up the rooms so no one would drive home drunk and would have a place to crash rather than drive drunk and Dillon had used them more than once despite living so close. He always carved a notch from the wood around the bed every time he stayed the night there.

Over the years Dillon had convinced Thad to reinforce everything in the massive structure under the mirage of added security. Thad had given his friend Dillon a budget and left the experienced man in charge of the security while occasionally helping with the physical parts of improving the security of the old bar. Dillon had been greatly compensated with free booze rather than cash for this job.

Kirtland D. Neal

"Hey Thad. How've y'all been?" Dillon asks as he goes up to the bar to see Thad while his friends sit down in his favorite booth. He notices a bit of stress on his friends face as he leans over the bar, propping himself up on both arms.

"We've been good, brother. I've been better though. You hear my little Sonia is trying to go on her first date?" He began as he pulled two glasses and a bottle out from under the bar. The furrow in his brow growing more prominent with every word. "Like man, I don't know what to do. I don't think that she should be allowed to date but Jill, well she keeps telling me to let her go. What do you think man?" the burly giant of a man seemed so vulnerable as he faced the same dilemma the befalls every girl's father.

Despite the sullen look on Thad's face Dillon can't help but to laugh a little bit. "Little Sonia?" he asks with crinkle of his nose. He lets his amusement slip out as he says the word little. "Thad, she's 17 years old man. To be honest brother I'm impressed you kept it from happening this long." He says cracking up a bit more as they down the shots that Thad had poured. Tequila. And it was a double shot of the good shit. Dillon turns so his back is resting against the bar, now only his elbows touched the bar top. "What I would do man," he says with a lot of hand movement. "Is I would take him out back and show him a few of your guns and make it clear if he gets more than a hug in, he might regret it. Maybe show him how accurate you can be with a knife or something silent." He suggests while waving the second shot in the air as he speaks, his free hand throwing an imaginary knife. They down the second and final round of shots as Dillon finishes talking.

Upon hearing this Thad perks up noticeably. All the tension which had previously riddled his face is now gone. A news headline coming across the tv screen catches Dillon's attention as he turns back towards Thad.   "For fuck's sakes man, another one?" Dillon exclaims. Thad turns to see the

Apocalypse Virus: Initial Infection
headline on the tv claiming the emergence of a new disease with
the potential to surpass COVID-19 and all the others of the last
few decades.

"I feel like we just finished dealing with one a few years
ago." Thad mutters sullenly. Dillon lets out a big sigh.

"I guess we should be used to this shit by now. Every other
month its some new disaster threatening us." They both shrug,
accepting the chaos of the modern world.

"Alright, thanks man. Y'all enjoy your lunch and I will
make sure to give you an extra discount." He begins cleaning the
glasses and the counter before Dillon has a chance to peel himself
from the bar.

"You know she won't be happy to hear that you are giving
your friends discounts, again right?" Dillon asks against his better
judgment, although he is sure he knows the impending reply.

"She can be upset until she turns red in the face and passes
out brother. I own the place and won't go broke from letting some
friends get some perks for helping me out with shit. Besides who
says she's going to see it?" The big man laughs out. He then
waves away his friend. "Now go eat before I change my mind."

Having reassured Thad with a teenage romance battle plan
Dillon goes to join his friends at the booth. It is the corner booth
closest to the stairwell door and has old red fabric that makes it
look like it had once been in a fancy restaurant. And the table had
been some college kid's art project. The base and long trunk were
countless keys all heated and held together while the table top
itself was metal rimmed wood table imbued with sea glass and

bottle caps. The booth could fit seven people, comfortably anyways. Jill, Thad's wife, comes over and takes their orders after Dill sits down.

"The usual D?" Jill ask rhetorically while writing down Dillon's order before he could reply. Her question more of formality than anything else. He almost always got the same thing, a pressed Cuban sandwich and two papas rellenas'. He would crack the rellenas open and dowse them in hot sauce and wash the whole meal down with an ice cold beer. It was one of his favorite meals he could get and was an added reason he loved his home city. "And what about you boy's then?" she asks gazing up from her note pad, the tip of her pen hovering just centimeters from where she stopped writing. Jill stands there in the same expecting pose that your mother would stand in when she was waiting for you make up your mind so she could resume whatever it was she was doing before you bothered her. A stance full of both affection and irritation. A stance Dillon had seen her take many times with both Thad and Sonia. And with well, almost everyone who entered this place. She is left standing there for a few minutes more before PB looks up from his tall laminated menu and begins ordering, and one after another the others follow suit.

"It feels like I haven't been here with all you guys in forever man." Lucas says as Jill walks away with their orders.

"I know dude. You haven't been able to come down since my dad's funeral." Dillon says somberly, "Shit bro. It's already been, what four years next month? It feels like just yesterday the five of us and my dad were raising hell at Tyler's wedding." The table sits there a moment or so staring at their mugs thinking back to both his brother's wedding and his dad's funeral which took place the following year. They had shared a lot of happiness and sadness. Dillon seemed to be the lynch pin that held the group together though. The others, through no fault of their own, had all gotten busy with life and would lose track of each other. Every few months though Dillon would check up on them and hang out with at least one of them and tried to keep tabs on everyone.

They all raise their glasses in another toast. "To family gained and family lost. Joined not by blood, but rather by loyalty to each other and those closest to each other." Dillon utters as they all echoed in unison.

Chapter 2

Tampa, Florida

Dillon Thompson

Dillon's lunch with the guys was great. They must have spent at least an hour or so just talking shit and laughing after they finished their food. Eventually they forced themselves away from the bar so they could walk the four blocks back to Dillon's apartment. There they had another round or two of beers and swapping stories as none of them were quite ready to return to their everyday lives, for this was one of those days they hoped would never end. The past few days however, they will be lucky to remember.

Unfortunately for them, all good things must come to an end.

"Today is a day surrounded by old friends and good spirits." Dillon says raising his shot glass as he begins a toast, the others following suit. "But like any good concert or party must end, so must this joyous reunion. This is the last round. I know you all have lives to get back too." They all begin to laugh for a second, they had always found it funny and at times useful that Dillon had such a way with words. He had helped them take home many women over the years with that silver tongue of his. "And in case I don't see y'all again, my brothers. Nothing could ever change that, we are all brothers. I expect all of you to bring your asses back down here before another four years passes." He finishes with a wink towards Luke. "To brothers!" they almost sing as they down a double shot of tequila.

"And to family, be they blood or otherwise, both living and alive in memory." they all rang out clanging their glasses together like they always did before once again parting ways. The guys knocked back the second round of shots, no salt or limes here. In all their cases it could be said that 'Mama ain't raise no bitch.' They chased it with one last beer before reluctantly getting their stuff and making the descent towards the street, one of the rare occasions Dillon ever took the elevator.

It isn't until they were downstairs saying goodbye to each other that Dillon feels a wave of uneasiness wash over himself. A subtle shiver sweeping up through his entire body from his toes to his head. He is initially unsure what to feel in the face of this uneasiness, not sure what to accredit it to. It is not until he clasped Lucas's hand and brings him in for a bro hug that Dillon realizes what it is. It is a sense that makes him feel like he might not see some or all these guys again. That feeling you have at the end of Senior year just after graduation. The heavy uncertainty as to whether you will manage to keep those high school friends in your life as you all move on to bigger and better adventures.

But that's crazy right? Dillon begins telling himself. *How can a person have a premonition of what might happen in the future, I mean they can't?* He struggles to calm himself, even managing not to display his anxiousness. A skill he has long since mastered at this point in his life. *And besides anything can happen in a few years, hell anything can happen in a day. So why do I feel more worried than when I left my parents' house to go overseas on all those deployments?* Dillon is struggling to comprehend why he feels so on edge. Trying and failing to convince himself everything will be fine. *I'm sure it's nothing, I'm just growing nervous about the future. Could this be a warning sign for an approaching midlife crisis? I will be 39 this year after all.*

His mind reels at the change in direction of thought. One domino of thought falling and crashing into another, taking his mind on a roller coaster of ideas. He had grown use to this dance at an incredibly early age. His mind now drifted away from thoughts of concern and foreboding to thoughts of his own legacy or lack thereof. *No, you're just being weird again* He tells himself as the guys finish their goodbyes and packing the luggage back into the two cars. For a moment he is lost in his own thoughts of foreboding. He looks up just in time to see them all zip off in the two vehicles. One heading to Tampa International airport. The other starting its slow and steady trip around the bay to the southern end of Hillsborough County.

Waving goodbye to his closest friends for what may very well be the last time. He stands at the side of the street as he watches them make their way down the busy streets of downtown Tampa and around the corner joining the countless other individuals who were caught in the enraging gridlock of afternoon rush hour slowly creeping forward towards their collective goal of home, wherever that might be for each individual. He turns and heads back up to his apartment as his friends maneuver the parking lot that was the interstate. As he ascends the stairs towards his place, he can't shake that uneasy feeling. It's almost like that nagging feeling you get when you know you have forgotten something, yet you can't remember what it is. By the time he gets up the stairs and is opening his front door he has convinced himself that he is over thinking things as he does everything and is simply being sentimental and paranoid.

It's not until Dillon sits down after finishing a few hours of cleaning that he is reminded of just how exhausting it is partying and hanging out with these guys. Well in fairness it was Dillon who always insisted on going harder than most people usually went. His aching body reminds him he is no longer the young 20 something year old man he used to be. He's sitting on the only unsullied spot on the couch, the fact that one even exists is a bona fide miracle. While sipping a new beer he stares out past all the trash bags and the newly cleaned window, gazing out at the beautiful sunset over Tampa Bay.

As he's blankly looking at this post card scene, he begins thinking about how his life led up to here. A sense of nostalgia which is no doubt brought on because of his earlier sense of unease. He has never considered himself a special or incredibly talented individual. He was smarter than a lot of people growing up but always too lazy to apply himself and try most of the time. Hell, he wasn't sure if he was graduating high school or not until a month after he walked across the stage at graduation. He received his diploma in the mail a few weeks later like the other delinquents he went to school with who were consistently in trouble or skipping school. *Man, Mom and Dad were so pissed of those last few months.* He laughs at himself remembering their fury at his obvious lack of concern about it all.

He had a 2.85 unweighted GPA, and he was amazed it got that high considering how little effort he afforded school. Four years on the swim team that never amounted to anything amazing other than a strong group of friends whom he rarely ever saw or spoke to after he graduated and moved away. Three long, hot summers as a lifeguard and camp counselor at a boy scout camp. He met his first love there. He had somehow managed four years without getting kicked out of the JROTC program they had at the school, never sure of why he joined, even less sure as to why he stayed. That was the extent of what he had managed to "accomplish" during his blurry high school career.

      While nothing he ever did growing up seemed to amount to anything significant, he always tried to enjoy himself and knew how to bend the rules and cut corners all to simply have a good time. That was always what he was the best at, having a good time and making sure others did too. No small feat considering his anxiety and depression which would cause him to suddenly leave parties because he just couldn't deal with people anymore for the day. The booze, sex, and drugs helped him to deal with his *'damage'* as he called it. There was never any logic to that part, there seldom was with mental illness. And while he may question why he did some of it, he has never for a second had any regrets for what he had done in the first 18 or so years of his life. And despite this carefree and irresponsible childhood he enjoyed he went and joined the Air Force after high school. Everyone was shocked when this most irresponsible and laziest person they knew decided to enlist. Truth be told it had been the only way he could see himself getting to leave Florida before he expected to overdose by his mid-twenties.

      He spent nine months after graduating working at a golf course cleaning up golf carts while he passed time waiting to leave for basic military training. He tried to flirt with ever cougar he came across, finding very quickly the fine line between a joke and honesty. His naturally flirtatious personality helped others be more receptive to his half truthful jokes.

      The first year in the military sucked ass like it sucks for everyone. For many it's the first time living away from their families and friends, first time dealing with that much responsibility. He lost count of how many days he would lay in his barrack room after work depressed, crying. Nor could he remember how often he had either thought of or attempted suicide, nothing drastic enough or obvious enough to draw unwanted attention to his mental well-being or lack thereof. It got drastically easier as time went on though. It got to a point with in the third year where he was legitimately happy for what felt life the first time in his life. A fleeting bliss.

He retired almost a year ago after twenty years in. Being a man just under 40 and being retired is an odd thing. He made it about ten days of being retired before he had to leave Arizona or risk going mad from boredom.

After cleaning out all of his stuff from his home in Arizona he moved into his Tampa apartment, which he had gotten six years prior. Renting it out as an Air B'n'B for the most part until he moved back. The apartment was roughly 30 or 40 minutes away from his parents' old house where they had moved after he graduated to finish raising his younger brothers. Despite being so close he found it hard to bring himself over that way, his parents' passing had only made things worse. His youngest brother, Sam now lived in the house with his wife and two kids. Once again, they were all amazing, it was Dillon who was the issue. His brother's, Tyler, Chris, and Sam were all use to it and knew that Dillon didn't mean anything by being so distant, it's just how he is and always has been. Although the three of them had had many lengthy discussions over the fact that since he had gotten back from his first deployment all those years ago, he seemed so much farther away than before, and the distance only worsened as the years went on. They all knew that he was always there for them should they need him though. Yet for Dillon it had always felt like he was walking along the edge of a dark pit, only a misstep from falling into complete darkness.

This was his first New Year's party as a civilian, so naturally he had done a lot of things he couldn't do while in the military, drugs mostly. Seems most people in the military look forward to those little freedoms once they get out. Everything is legal now, as oppose to when he was growing up so many years ago. To be more specific he had smoked a metric shit ton of weed, and a good amount of cocaine. Marijuana had been nationally legalized for medical and recreational use almost shortly after he enlisted, but it was still illegal according to the Uniform Code of Military Justice.

He never did it since he actually wanted to keep his job and not get discharged. Now he has become close friends with Red, the owner of Reggae Red's Cannabis Store a block or two past Pete's. He grows his own supply, so he has better prices on his stuff than the other guys around here.

Dillon now spends his days teaching tourist to sail boats and sailboard when he needs to make a bit of drinking money or just wants to keep busy, but he has no need of a job. He was making more money than he knew what to do with from the stocks. Whatever came into his bank account from stocks after the $50,000 mark was thrown into some real estate investments. Spending crazy money to turn around, reinvest it and make even crazier money. He has his retirement fund just bulking up since he can't touch it until he turns 65.

He has way more money than he knows what to do with. He has already traveled the world a few times over. The hard part now is trying to figure out what to do with all the money. He has been reinvesting roughly a quarter of all his profits. He has this pimped out apartment and numerous more homes and hideouts all over the world. All of them paid in cash because who needs a good credit score when they have this much paper. Same thing with all his vehicles. All the utilities and upkeep cost came out automatically so he wouldn't have to think about it all. He paid for his parents' house before they passed away. He gave it to Sam and his wife as a ten-year wedding anniversary present after their parents' affairs had been settled. Now he buys small companies and make large donations to his old school and some other

charities. He even managed to buy his own island in the
Caribbean.

He enjoys teaching people to sail, it is something he has
always enjoyed since he first learned as a teenager. And for many
years all he wanted to do was live on a sailboat. It didn't hurt that
it always helped him to impress many women over the years, as
well as a few guys. After his birthday this May he intends on
sailing off and spend a few years traveling and living in his 50-
foot sailboat, the Speciem *Maris*. Which in Latin is roughly
translated to *Beauty of the Sea*. He has had her for a little over 15
years now and has never been as happy as he is when he's out on
the ocean miles from shore. The coastline no more than a blurry
dot in the vast sapphire jewel of an ocean. Not a soul around, just
him, the ocean, and the creatures who call the sea home.

That may be why he has never stayed with any of the
women he was in love, because the allure of the sea in all her
majesty has ruled over his heart and soul since he was a young
child. Perhaps it was just a condition of growing up in Florida.
There were however a few women who had managed to steal his
time and affection more than the sea yet had left him in one way
or another, pushing him closer to the foamy white tops of the
choppy waves crashing over themselves as they came ever nearer
to shore before once again returning to the deep ocean. With each
thrust out to the deep blue waters he found it increasingly difficult
to return, his humanity slowly eroded and dragged out to sea
leaving only a jagged cliff face of the man he once was.

Chapter 3

Tampa, Florida

January 3rd, 2030

Sometime just after Midnight

Dillon had fallen asleep whilst thinking of the ocean and his upcoming odyssey. The dreams he is currently having are some of the best he has ever had or will ever have. The world has fallen away to leave him on his boat in the middle of the sea, no sight of land any direction. A strong headwind coaxing the vessel ever onwards towards an undetermined destination. The waves and wind roar in Dillon's ears as they rush past, a friendly conversation between old lovers. His only companions are the dolphins which race along with him. Playing in the sun, breaking the surface before crashing down mere moments later. Even these majestic creatures are subject to Gravity's whim. His feet thoughtlessly dance across the deck of the sailboat, adjusting sails and lines on muscle memory and instinct. The entire choreography is as effortless as it appears. Sailing with the same ease with which most people would walk. After decades of sailing and teaching others the same this bare foot ballroom dance is one of the most natural things to him. Like sleeping or breathing.

Apocalypse Virus: Initial Infection

He is abruptly awoken from his drunken dreams by a deafening explosion far off. He bolts upright at the noise on red alert, for an eternity of a moment he is back in the center of a hell he once thrived in. The lack of assault rifle by his side proves a fierce enough reminder of where he truly is. Quickly calming down, he simply sits there wiping the sleep out his eyes as he sits there in the now darkened apartment. A thunderous heart rate blocks out all other sounds for an instant. The half a beer he had fallen asleep with was now soaked into the carpet at his feet. A few drops held onto the lip of the bottle in classic Mufassa style, no Scar's to throw them off. The bottle lay on its side pointing out the back window, as if to say ' look, there's danger over there'.

Angrily mumbling incoherently under his breath, Dillon grabs the now mostly empty bottle and stumbled into the kitchen to throw it away.

"Aw what the hell now?!" he hisses as he realizes the power is out, again. He flicks the light switch on and off to try and get the lights to come on as it is now dark. He is answered with nothing more than dim moonlight to guide him through his apartment. A simple task which would have proven impossible not even twenty-four hours prior.

"Those god damn college kids blew the power for the building again." He was thinking that Bobby and Casey, two college dropouts, were throwing another crazy party down the hall. The parties didn't bother Dillon, in fact he would often stop in for a while and party himself. What he did have a problem with was when they caused the power to go out, which happened at least twice a month. And Dillon, having electrical experience throughout his first few years in the military, was usually the one that would fix the power outage. The building manager was an incompetent fuck as far as Dillon was concerned. The tripped breakers were child's play for him, even occasionally having to replace one or repairing an electrical line were extremely simple. Dillon's efforts were often rewarded with free booze or pizza from the dropouts since it would save them any ass pain from the building manager. Since he had retired, they started adding edibles to the rotation.

After fumbling around for his flip flops, tools and parts he heads for the stairs, but not before beating on the guys' door. A few minutes pass of him waiting and knocking before Bobby Fisher opens the door, half asleep himself. Bobby finds an aggravated Dillon standing outside his door dressed in cargo shorts and a tattered tank top. Toolbox and a new beer on the floor next to Dillon's feet.

"What's up man?" The stoner groggily inquires, his face twisted in confusion and drowsiness. He had clearly been up for a little while, not long but long enough to have rubbed the sleep off his face.

"Wait, you guys aren't having another party?" Dillon asks. All lividity rapidly replaced with much greater confusion as he viewed the darkened apartment that looked like someone had been asleep moments before, which Bobby probably was enjoying another drug fueled slumber. The potency of today's strain still clouded the man and his residency. Bobby wordlessly shakes his head. "Then do you have any idea what made the power go out this time?"

"I don't know bro but like the whole city has run dark dude. Casey woke me up when it happened about an hour ago. And look," he said pulling up his phone to show Dillon that he had no service, none of the apps would even launch. They were coming up with errors. "Like what's happening man? Where did all the power go? Who broke the internet?"

Apocalypse Virus: Initial Infection

"I don't know Bobby. You said your brother woke you up an hour or so ago?" the baffled kid nodded. "What the hell was that explosion a few minutes ago?" This question seemed to spark life into some sort thought train which had been dormant a moment before.

"There's people tearing shit apart on the streets. It was a car…I think." He opened the door wide enough for Dillon to have a clear line of sight to the windows. "See the faint red glow along the bottom of the window? That's the glow of the fires they've lit as they have been destroying everything." Dillon was starting to get a twisted knot in the pit of his stomach, hoping he was wrong but fairly sure he wasn't. His heart rate is starting to climb as his thoughts race through all the possibilities. None of which are good.

"Alright just stay inside until I come back with and answer. And don't answer if you don't know the person." As much as those two idiots pissed him off, he treated them like little brothers. Dillon walks back into his apartment as the eerie feeling that had consumed him yesterday returns. He looks out the still dirty window and sure as shit the normally illuminous city skyline was near pitch black darkness with nothing more than reflected moonlight to outline the buildings. It was a rare sight of beauty to see the Tampa sky as this peaceful silhouette, the far-off ocean melting into the starry night sky. He stans there a second to take in the new view, still oblivious to what had really caused the black out. He glances down as he takes in the red glow and the chaos of the looters.

A clamor rises from the streets below, snapping him out of his distracted train of thought. Dillion grows ever more warry of what he might find while he searches for the truth behind the blackout.

He makes his way through the apartment under the guidance of his flashlight. He quickly changes into his combat boots, jeans, and a shirt with his Kevlar vest tossed over it. He figured it was better to have it and not need it than the other way around. He hurries through the residency as he grabs his S&W 500 Magnum revolver out of the table nearest the entry way. Tucks his two dagger boot knives, 440 blade Elk Ridge diving knife, and a Ka-bar in their various sheaths while he stashes a simple pocketknife away in his pocket. He throws a small first aid bag over one shoulder, so the strap lay diagonally across his torso. He barely remembers to grab the Model 870 TAC-14 shotgun he kept leaning behind his nightstand. With that slung over his other shoulder he is ready for damn near anything.

Having changed and armed himself he makes his way down through the large stairwell, the only light in there coming from the battery power emergency exit lights and the mag light in his left hand.

He tells the few familiar faces who peak out, to go back into their apartments until he can make sure it is safe for them to come down. He tells Frank, the door man, to lock up all the entrances and only let residents back inside the building. The young man quickly scuttles off to follow his orders without question. His time in the building had earned him enough good faith for everyone to respond well and listen to him.

What awaits Dillon on the street is something he had never hoped to see in the states. For an instance he feels as though he is having a flash back to when one of the black hawks that was transporting him and his unit over Syria had its tail rotor shot to shit by some soviet era RPG which somehow managed to hit them and even more unlikely didn't kill them on impact. The pilots were able to guide and ease the crash with the main rotor enough for everyone to jump out with minimal injuries before the bird slammed into the ground, become a twisted mound of flaming scrap after the blades fractured off and went flying in multiple directions. None the less they still landed in some ISIS controlled village at the base of some mountains in central Syria. The dozen crash survivors were forced to fend off and avoid the enemy for a few hours until their rescue came. The sight that laid out before him, like a nightmare, looked so much like an urbanized version of the brutal war he had fought in. He sees cars on fire, people looting and committing countless violent acts in the name of fear or maybe just reckless abandon. This is no surprise, people always seem to lose their minds a little bit when put in an apparent time of crisis, especially now a day's.

It seems after the Baltimore riot about 15 years ago and then the Trump scandal several years ago everyone has been on edge, even with the new president in office things have still been very tense. Lord knows the police haven't been a comfort to the people of America in a long time. Dillon had learned at an early age that no matter what else may be said about a person three things hold true. They're able to be brutally evil, genuinely benevolent, and are full of limitless potential to become greater than they are. Be it a greater menace or a greater force of compassion and kindness. He always saw these three things in everyone. But what he saw now was simply uncensored, primal chaos. Not only were these people being violent, but some were falling over writhing in agony and screaming so primitively and painfully that it made even this seasoned veteran shiver with pity and fear. It is like they were so dreadfully ill. He thinks he sees their skin bubbling, boiling in their own body. He has to be imagining it, or so he tells himself.

Dillon struggles to fight off the fit of PTSD that is clawing it's way to the surface, coming forth as though beckoned by the present chaos and calamity. A demon drawn to the feelings of a hellish reality. He is snapped back to attention by a pair of younger guys slowly approaching him from across the street with a glint of evil in their eyes and smiles devoid of anything good. He sees their mouths moving in what was likely trash talk, he is unable to hear them through the deafening clamor in his ears. The one on the left looks maybe late 20's. He is light skinned in a way that you aren't sure what race he was or where he's from. He wears some dirty old Nike's, freshly blood splattered jeans a few sizes too big that barely stayed above his knees and a stained old tank top. He has a baseball bat with nails hammered and bent in the fat end, the old blood coating it told Dillon that this guy wasn't anywhere near a saint on a regular day, let alone today. The shine over parts of the dried blood looked fresh. He would surely be trouble.

The man next to him looks a few years younger, his little brother or cousin maybe? They look similar despite being dressed so differently. The younger one has on some dimly shining dress shoes, dirty black slacks, and a white button up halfway undone and partially untucked, and black tie which seemed to be plastered to his skin because of the sweat, blood, and grime. He looks kind of like waiter who had lost his shit at work. He drags a bloodied red axe, like the ones used in case of fires. It scrapes against the asphalt behind him so loudly that everything else seems to fade away but the sound of metal against road. Every few steps a spark comes off of the metal being raked along the road. Any ounce of dread, fear, or anxiety drains from Dillon as he takes a few deliberately slow steps forward before stopping and cracking his neck and back. Now Dillon is excited, he hasn't been in a fight like this since he came back from his last deployment. A fight which is clearly life or death from the onset. His Adrenal Medullas begins pouring adrenaline into his blood, kicking every muscle fiber into turbo. He won't bring out the gun if he doesn't have to, its more enjoyable this way for him. So, he plucks out his Ka-bar and tucks his light into his back pocket. With his free right hand, he opens and closes his hand as if to say *Come and get some boys!* He flips the knife in his hand a few times in impatience.

Apocalypse Virus: Initial Infection
    The older one with the bat starts to run forward, the younger one stays back choosing to allow his brother to have some fun first.

Chapter 4

Summerfield Technical Solutions
Bio-med R&D facility E-5
Somewhere in the Florida Everglades

August 25th, 2029
Several months ago

Tabitha Jones, a young woman fresh of her master's degree for Microbiology, had been ecstatic when she landed this gig with STS six months ago. She was still a little mystified that this technological titan. A company which had been revolutionizing not just science, but almost everything about life. This same super company had chosen her, a 25-year-old with average grades who had served internships at several small labs and hospitals. They chose this young woman from a small town in southern Oregon to fill a slot for a job that people with Doctorate's degrees had been turned down for.

What is so special about this seemingly average young scientist? What was it that would make her qualified to fill such a position? She only filled out the application after her boyfriend and professor had both nagged her to apply for weeks. She never expected to get the job even then. But sure, enough about the time she had forgotten about it she got called in to the STS administrative building close to the University of San Diego. She had originally thought it was a friend prank calling her. But the call and interview all turned out to be legit. And three weeks after finishing her degree she was moving out to south Florida to work at this hidden research lab. Her and Jeff, her now ex-boyfriend, had broken up because they, or rather he, couldn't handle the long distance and their jobs were both too important.

Tabitha is gazing off into the distance, her expression resembles that of someone trying to work out a rather difficult problem. She is waiting for a test to finish running on yet another new chemical. She is trying to remember the last time she saw her family. She didn't even have time to go back home to see them before she had to move across the country. It has now been a few years since she was home. Part of her hated going home just to find that most everyone she knew was still doing pretty much the same thing that they all had been doing back in high school. It would confound her very existence how after she had changed, evolved so much that everyone else was simply stagnant. The only changes in those bleary small town lives was the occasional marriage and over frequent pregnancy.

Yet, even considering these hidden feelings of resentment there was a need. A desire to go back home in honor of all those amazing memories she had shared with her friends and family growing up. The empty pang of home sickness had become a constant variable a long time ago for her. To her it was something just in the back of her mind. Ignored for the most part like that tattoo she had gotten over her chest and shoulder. Essentially forgotten during the numerous and tolling hours of the day, just clawing to the surface for brief moments during those evenings sitting up late in her apartment. These falters of mental armor would result in anxiety attacks of varying degrees. Occasionally these shadowy assailants would strike her psyche in the bright of day and catch her off guard. Often leading to her having to ask for an early lunch or take a rather long bathroom break and claim that her crimson friend was making its monthly visit. Today was one of those bold attacks in the light, although this one seemed to take a more benign approach than the usual attacker.

Kirtland D. Neal

Tabitha sees the modest two-story burgundy house that her and her brother grew up in. The scent of fresh cut grass creeps forward. A phantom odor, alive only in her memory. There is the swing set that her dad had built hiding in the shade of the ancient oak which towers over the back yard. The swing set was by no means the nicest looking thing in the world, but it was sturdy and had grown over the years to captivate herself and Jackson, her younger brother. Jackson. He would be almost 21 now. She remembers the old family video of how excited she got when their parents had told them she was going to be a big sister. Her mom would always recount how from that first day he came home the way the two of them seemed to be inseparable. Even as they got older and she would seem to outgrow playing with and dressing up her younger brother she would still go out of her way to take care of him, even if he didn't see it that way. He usually did not see it that way. And through everything they would still tease each other and play tricks on one another. Sometimes dad would get in on the tricks and mom would try to be stern and yell at them all but would often end up losing it half way through her rant and they would all end up laughing so hard it was tough to breath. They were often a rather happy family.

The dull sound of laughter is broken by a deafening crack of snapping fingers. With a shake of her head her vision clears to find that she is still in the lab. There is a caramel colored hand hanging in the air just a few inches in front of her nose. As the hand falls back to the side of the person who had just held it there, she realizes what happened. She was snapped out her autopilot daydream by Ricco Argo, her closest work friend and a fellow lab tech. He had been at the lab for a few years before she arrived. He still treated her as an equal though. That is probably why they became such good friends so quickly.

"Hello, Earth to Tabi. Anyone home?" he chuckles waving his other hand back and forth in front of her face "Come on back to us. There you are," he says as she shakes off her immersive thoughts. "Where the hell do you always go Tabitha? Like seriously girl, you've got to stop doing the whole space cadet thing at work or go get a job with NASA." He turns back to his work besides her as she comes too.

"Sorry Ricco, just thinking." She begins to apologize, almost reflexively.

"Well no shit, Sherlock!" he snorts off, putting an end to any further explanation. He over exaggerates a painful moan as she punched his arm, admittedly harder than she had meant to. "Hey!" Rico playfully cries as he feigns being hurt, "I need that arm to work." He wails loudly as he grabs his arm as if it were dislocated or broken, a shit eating grin spread across his tan face.

"Don't be such an ass and you won't get hit as much. "she giggles, tongue darting out in a juvenile jest. "And I am still trying to figure out how a few seemingly average young people fresh off their graduate's degree managed to land such a cake gig like this. I mean at least I'm beautiful, but you?" she says playfully eyeing him up and down "I don't see why even a blind woman would hire your dumb ass." her left hand forms an L on her forehead

"Ouch! That was a low blow Jones, low even for you." He says grabbing his chest like he had been shot. "It's okay though, not everyone is susceptible to my devilish charm. You are among those select few who are immune so you can't see just how irresistible the rest of the planet finds me." A cocky grin spreads across his face.

"Whatever you idiot." She shrugs his words off as she pushes his face away.

This was how most of their nights at work went. The two of them talking and trading jokes and insults. Around 6 they would go the work café and usually get Chinese food, her Sesame chicken, pork dumplings, and lo mien, and him Mongolian beef and rice with egg rolls. then they would resume work in the lab for several more hours. Their work primarily consisted of mixing certain biological samples with different chemicals and run the through a battery of test to determine the viability of each sample. If the sample showed promise, they would begin testing the samples of various organisms, mostly mice and various plants. They were glorified beaker tweekers as Tabitha thought of it.

Since Tabitha had started working here several months before she had never seen a sample make it past the plants and mice. Yet despite the apparent failures they had still been told that they were doing a great job countless times by the bosses who would come through a few times a month. Even though it all seemed insignificant they were still held to strict rules of confidentiality and several non-disclosure agreements. Tabitha had just thought they were being optimistic and paranoid. Supposedly nothing of value had come out of this facility in the last three years. Nothing had even come out of the southeast of the US in the last year or two that made any money, yet still money flowed into to several facilities like this one. And despite how pointless much of it seemed Tabitha enjoyed the simple lab work and running the various calculations and creating all sorts of formulae. It was essentially a playground to experiment with whatever she wanted.

It didn't matter what results they wielded as the company view every failure as a valuable lesson on what doesn't work. And rumor had it that all the samples that were fatal were sold to the CDC and militaries for a pretty hefty price. Tabitha had created about a dozen or so samples herself that had made it to the live testing, and one or two that seemed to have initial success with the mice, the mice made it two weeks without any complications and had actually seemed to overcome their deficiencies for a little while, but suddenly they all just died. That was about a month ago.

Ever since then she had been tweaking and adjusting the serum to try and eliminate the death sequence that so far seemed inevitable. Tonight, she was working on what she was calling K-55. She chose K for Kryptonite, since the serum seemed to give the subjects a super immune system and she was a huge comic book geek. The goal for this one was to create a substance that could overcome any sort of defect that a person might have. A defect in this case would be anything such as chronic and terminal diseases, allergies, degenerative diseases, some mental illnesses, physical handicaps. She was hoping to eliminate these with cellular regeneration as a means to regrow any damaged or dead cells, even to the level to regrow a missing limb or replace the brain cells lost due to severe head trauma that plagued many athletes.

Basically, she was trying to create a miracle drug that acted as a catch 22 and treated everything that could ail a person, even trivial things such as nearsightedness. So far it had managed to regrow brain and nerve cells, and a few subjects had overcome allergies to various things. And Dave the mouse had managed to regrow part of a missing toe but was still missing an entire leg. But no matter how promising they had all looked, they all died. Today she was replacing the bacteria that she had been using with an artificial virus that she had made a couple of months ago. By the end of the day she has successful simulations on the computer program, which is music to her ears. It also means that tomorrow will be another round of new plant and mice test.

She locks her stuff in her cabinet before leaving to go return to her tiny one-bedroom apartment about thirty minutes away. Her Pomeranian, Michelangelo, eagerly awaits her return from work as he does every day. She sets her bag and keys down on the table next to the front door. She continues walking, flicking the lights on in her small kitchen, as she grabs the dog food and pours it into Angelo's bowl and refilling his water. She plops down with a bottle of cheap beer on the tattered old leather couch her parents had given her after high school. She stared off in the distance at no spot in particular on the wall. She had painted it a sandy brown to bring out a warm feeling in the confined space.

As she so often does, she lets her thoughts drift off to the past. Reliving all the adventures her and her friends had gotten into in high school and college. She was still amazed that they all survived all the stupid shit they did growing up like the time they all climbed to the high school roof drunk off their asses. Then standing two stories up all jumped into the swimming pool beneath the glass covered roof top. And they were naked on top of it all. They had all somehow managed to avoid getting arrested in high school.

She is startled from her nostalgia by a fuzzy orange weight hopping into her lap and licking her face. "I missed you to baby." She chuckles as she cuddles the affectionate dog for a moment or two before flipping on Netflix. She watches some documentary on how 2010 to 2020 forever changed the world, for good and bad. Mostly bad. Sometime later she dozes off learning about world altering events from her childhood. Blissfully unaware of what is happening not too far away. What might single handedly change all of life.

Chapter 5

Tampa, Florida

Dillon

     Bat-dude comes rushing forward as he feverously swings the bat side to side. There's obviously no method to his madness. No style or technique. Dillon barely side steps the bat in time to dodge it before kicking the side of this dude's knee cap. This rewards him with a sickening crunch and the guy falls wailing and clutching his knee. His knee is visibly destroyed as his lower leg almost dangles from the thigh at an unnatural angle. If this guy by some miracle survives this fight, he will definitely be crippled.

     The man who is wielding the axe now charges forward screaming with the rust speckled blade clutched with both hands high above his head. He swings with a reservoir of pent up rage, the motion is so sloppy, slow, and predictable that Dillon has no problem avoiding the axe. The weapon sinks promptly into a wrecked impala. Axe-man is struggling to dislodge the blade from the hood of a car he just hit. Grunting as his muscles strain when all his effort goes unrewarded. He is still being driven more by aggression than fear at this point, oblivious to everything but his current task of dislodging the axe. He doesn't hear Dillon until he feels the knife slice open his throat. Axe-man's eyes grow wider than hubcaps milliseconds before he falls forward uselessly holding his throat trying to slow the bleeding. His efforts prove to be of no avail. Warm blood squirts out between his hands, the warm blood flowing over the hands of both men. Moments later he lay in a growing puddle of blood. Dead.

After quickly dislodging the axe from the punctured front end of the impala Dillon makes his way over to the other guy trying to stand up on his one good leg. The now crippled man appears terrified after what he has just witnessed. Despite the immense fear growing inside of him he can't manage to utter a single word. Not even as Dillon slams the axe through the top of his skull, the action accompanied by an audible thud and muffled crunch. Blood ebbs out from the wound, coating the blade in a fresh layer of gleaming crimson before cascading down over the man's head in all directions.

Dillon looks up and catches his reflection in the glass of a nearby building. Beneath the blood splatter that now covers him is a dark, non-expressive face. Its beyond stoic with his cold, cruel, and calculating eyes. A slight furrow in his brow. He finds that he looks a great deal older and meaner than he recalled looking. His lips are curled up slightly on one side to form a devilish smirk, the smile of a man who relished in being bad like this. Despite his outward appearance he is flooded with emotion for a moment or two as he gazes upon the still warm corpses. He struggles to identify the feeling at first, it is something he hasn't felt in a while. Pity. He looks at what is left of the two strangers with pity, for if they had never tried to attack him, they might still be alive. A shadowy feeling lay just below the pity. A darker side of him feels a surge of pride and power. His blood speeds up, darkened by this malicious persona. This is the version of himself that loves the fight to live on. In a way there is no greater death than to die fighting, at least in his eyes. Second best was to die doing something or someone that you loved. Both were deaths with meaning to him. This is the darkness he has kept hidden from the rest of the world. His own cruel beast which he constantly struggles to keep locked away. *Is the demon's cage broken for good?* He wonders, unsure of how much this night may affected him.

After scavenging what he can from the bodies he continues his way down the street which seems to be clearing as the tide of anarchy flows to other streets. One of the few people remaining on the street is a woman running away from three men. She is running right towards Dillon. *Turn around and walk away.* He tells himself *"It's not your fight dammit, just go back inside."* Despite this he moves ever faster to the fleeing women, his walk speeds up to a jog. *"You dumbass!"* He yells in his head as he realizes how much bigger these guys are as they get closer. Dillon slows to a standstill as he hides the women behind him, trying to shield her from the troublesome trio, who has now stopped and is standing about a dozen feet in front of him with the same evil looks as Axe-man and bat-boy.

One of them is still in mechanic outfit, the apron pulled down to his waist exposing the white shirt underneath, a massive monkey wrench in his right hand. He easily weighted in at over 240lbs and is clearly taller than Dillon is. The one to his left is in paint covered clothes and just as big as the mechanic. This one is wielding a hefty old crowbar. Their other friend is just as massive as the other two. He is in cargo shorts that hung on him as if they were a size or two too big for him, stopping well below the knee. His plaid shirt was also excessively large on him with the bottom ends of a white shirt jutting out beneath it to cover his waistline. He is the only one not in work boots, instead rocking some well-maintained timberland boots which are more for show than function.

He is wielding an old, classic looking machete. The crown and trident tattoos on each of their arms and the gold bandanas made it evidently clear to Dillon that the trio of giants before him were Latin Kings. Dillon spots a faded Mi Vida Loco tattoo on the mechanic's hand. A sign of the gangster having served some time. They may be poorly armed gangsters but are gangsters non the less. Dillon is congratulating himself on yet another incredible feat of stupidity, mentally rolling his eyes at himself.

"Hey there fellas. Lovely night for a walk huh?" he waves casually.

"Shut it gringo!" the Mechanic yells back.

"Well now. That is no way to treat a stranger," he chimes with a cheery and sarcastic tone while his hands are raised as if it might stop the rudeness, the axe still in one hand. "Now what would your mother say if she heard you talking to someone you just met like that?" clearly not the best thing to say. They seem to all get fed up with him in the same moment as they move from their spots. *"Fuck."* Dillon really doesn't want to fight these three like he had the last two, especially with a crying woman cowering behind him. He is too exhausted and out muscled. They start too close in on the several feet remaining between them. Dillon knows he can't easily get the shotgun strapped to his back out in front of him before they pounced on him, but he remembered what he has tucked up in his waistband as his hand brushes against the 500 Special. Never dropping his upbeat performance despite how screwed he thinks he is "I promise; you guys really don't want to do this." They move faster with bigger grins. They by no means look like scholars, or even the top 100 of the class but they are smart enough to know they have him out numbered. "Alright, I tried to warn you." He says shaking his head as he drops the axe and pulls his revolver out. They barely have enough time to process the gun before it's over.

Bang! Bang! Bang! Bang! Bang!

Apocalypse Virus: Initial Infection

Dillon unloads the entire gun on them. The three men fall dead on the street there, weapons which had been in their hands go skittering across the pavement. The woman still shaking and burying her face into the back of his shirt. Putting the gun away he turns around to face the woman. She gazes out from behind him in confusion and glances over at the now cooling corpses. The events that just unfolded finally start registering with her as she tunes back into reality. Fear grabs hold of her as she catches a glimpse at the sidearm, he is tucking beneath his clothes and connects the dots. Dillon sees all this play out on her face within seconds. She goes to start running again but Dillon holds her against him in a fierce bear hug.

"Help!" shrieks the woman as Dillon turns her around to face him. "Let me go! Murderer!" she yells into his chest, somewhat muffled. She frantically carries on like this for a few minutes while she attempts to pummel his chest hoping to escape from him. She is clearly too worn out to put up too much of a fight, she still manages to rake her nails across Dillon's arms with enough force to break skin leaving reddening lines which gradually build up to a series of disconnected trickles of blood. She soon losses any remaining energy she has to fight as she stops her escape attempts ad her body grows lax.

"You done?" he asks, an eyebrow cocked up that she can't even see with her face still buried in his chest. She huffs in defeat and nods, "Alright now just relax alright, I'm one of the good guys alright." Dillon pauses as he awaits another sign of compliance. He doesn't have to wait more than a moment or so before she nods again. He puts on his best impression of a friendly firefighter just wanting to help.

"Now what's your name?" his hold loosens as she looks up with big glassy amber eyes, the makings of tears just sparkling on the lower edges as the woman is fighting back tears.

"Elizabeth, Elizabeth Taylor. You can call me Liz though." Says the woman, Liz, in a saddened, defeated voice clearly still unsure of how this will play out although it is the most viable possibilities presented before her. She is not about to tell him that though, and she doesn't have to it turns out.

"Well, Liz, do you have a place nearby?" Dillon inquires in the most genuine and codling voice he can muster, which on a good day is hard for him to manage. Today is far from a good day for him as you all might have figured out by now.

"No," she sniffles, tears begin to slide down her face as she tries to put on a brave face, more for herself than anything else. "I was on my way to the airport when everything went to hell." *Well, shit,* he thought to himself knowing what he was about to propose is a terrible idea, some might even wager it is the worst plan he could have made in that entire day. One that would very probably get him in even more trouble than he cared for. And most definitely cause him more pain than he was prepared for. Even knowing all this the dumbass still speaks against his better judgement.

"Do you want to come back to my apartment building and I can clean up that cut on your forehead?" he asks with a wince, not sure if he wants to hear the answer one way or another.

"Really? You would do that for me?" She eagerly perks up after he asked that. Under normal circumstances no one in their right mind would have gotten so excited at the offer to return to the home of a man who had just gunned down three men without hesitation or any sign of remorse. Usually that would lead them to run as far away as possible. These were anything but normal circumstances. The eve of the end of world as they knew it. He nods despite his better judgement.

"Yes! Oh, thank you so much!" Dillon ushers her towards his apartment building just a few hundred yards down the street. He keeps her right in front of him so he can keep an eye on her, still not sure what type of person she is. The freshly paired duo made it maybe a dozen feet or so in the direction of the building before Dillon notices how everything about the woman seemed oddly calm. She begins to fall forward a moment later as she collapses from stress and exhaustion. He quickly closes the four or five feet between them in a single stride and catches her, gently lowering her to the ground. A quick survey shows that she has no other wounds, or at least none that were on the surface or immediately life threatening. Dillon stands up for a moment as she lay on her back, her chest slowly rising and falling in a steady, sleepy rhythm. His piercing blue-grey eyes search the street in every direction, searching for more trouble. Dillon has never been more grateful for an empty street in his entire life. And yet a part of him was greatly disappointed when he is unable to find any more fun. He knows he is better off for the deserted street, carrying her would make him incredibly vulnerable and at a complete disadvantage if someone were to insist upon fighting him. The only people he could see on along the crumbling strip of road are either dead or so desperately wishing that they soon would be.

A voice in his head whispers something which is barely audible amidst all the red alerts and sirens that are going off in his mind. This faint thought is a simple one, a choice he can make and has made before. *Leave her here, she will get you killed.* He stands above her for what feels like an eternity as he debates what to do. He finds it impossible to peel his eyes from her placid, expressionless face while he concludes what he knew he from the beginning. He crouches down and picks her up in his arms. If she had been conscious the gesture may have been perceived as romantic. He carries her the rest of the way back home, stopping just long enough at the desk in the lobby to explain everything that had happened in the last thirty minutes to Frank.

After he takes her to his lofty apartment and treats her wounds, he makes sure to spread word throughout the building of what is happening outside. Dillon and several other men from all over the building join together to barricade the entrances to the building in order keep them and their families safe. Fred sets to work on creating a guard schedule to keep a constant eye on the entrances. After the barricades are up and in place Dillon returns to the nightmarish massacre which is sprawled out to either side of the road. He searches all the bodies he came across for weapons and anything else of value. He had to make several trips back to the front desk to deposit his stashes before he is finished collecting what he can. He drags all the bodies to a spot on one side of the street, right next to a pair of totaled cars. He rips the clothes of the deceased to create wicks to shove down the gas tanks. He lights the pile on fire and walks back inside. Burning the bodies is the best way he can think to deal with them in a way that might avoid spreading any diseases they came across.

After a few more hours of work Dillon has the building secured and running like a military complex. He is secretly proud of how easy it is to still run things like he used to. He would never admit it, but a small part of Dillon has missed this militaristic existence and is glad for the chance to do it. That is a small, like miniscule small, part of him. Especially now. The rest of him is simply glad to be safe, to rest for a few hours as he collapses onto his bed, fully clothed and far too exhausted to change that. His boot knives and diving knife still strapped in their holsters as he only bothered to remove the Ka-bar and handgun to allow him to lay on his back freely. They are on the nightstand a foot or so away from his head. He will have to remember to clean everything when he wakes up.

Apocalypse Virus: Initial Infection

He is awoken by the sounds of screaming and someone beating against a door. Or maybe it is a wall? Either way he is annoyed already. The faint light fighting its way past the curtains tells him it can't be too long after dawn. He grabs the 500 magnum and then thinks better and replaces it on the nightstand, grabbing the Ka-bar instead. His watch reads 0630. *Yay! Another three-hour night.* He sarcastically thinks to himself. He is sleepily stumbling his way out his bedroom door, now halfway between his bed and the guest room, when realization hits him like a freight train. The girl. He had locked her in the room to make sure she didn't do anything crazy when she woke. He tucks his ka-bar away as he realizes he won't need it. Now fully awake he rushes towards the door to unlock it. He opens the door and the banging stops. He doesn't get to say anything before a small fist connects with his cheek.

"Oh no! I am so sorry. First you saved me last night, then you put me in here to rest and then…." Her frantic apology is cut short. He grabs her wrist to remove the hand that is caressing his face, much like his mom used to when he would come home with a black eye or a bruise from a fight he had gotten in at school. He looks at her unfazed by the punch. She winces a little as he grips her wrist tighter and firmer than he meant to.

"It's me who should be apologizing. I only locked the door to keep both of us safe, didn't want you waking and up and freaking out…kind of like you did." He lets go of her wrist, both of their arms drop. His shoulders sag as he starts chastising himself for being such an idiot.

"No, you shouldn't be apologizing," Liz says gazing downward, too embarrassed to look at his face, "It was very kind of you to do all this for me, some stranger you don't even know. I don't know how I can ever repay you." He has a blank expression as he scratches his stubbly chin in a carefree manner as he thinks for a moment.

"Just leave as soon as all this shit on the street stops, and don't steal anything." He says walking away from the now dumb founded woman. She feels slightly infuriated by his request, but she doesn't know why since he's been so nice. "Nothing personal, it's simply better if I am alone. Safer that way." He doesn't look back as he continues walking. She can't see the faraway look in his eyes because he is turned away from her, but she can hear it. Hear the melancholy and bitterness in his voice as he utters that last sentence. She closes her mouth before she says anything.

She can feel that he has no ill will towards her, so she is no longer offended. The icy coldness of some deep and startling darkness emanates from him in those few moments. An eerie fog spilling out and over everything within its expanding radius. Liz can almost feel the weight of the ghost of his past as they bring about a rigidness to the air around him and the whole apartment. She lets him walk off as she lay back on the bed staring up at the ceiling, telling herself she should just follow his advice and not even attempt to get to know him. But no matter how long she tells herself that, some ever-growing part of her tells her that she needed to get to know him.

But why? I mean sure he's incredibly attractive, one might even say hot. She tells herself. *But there's something more than that. Something about the way he seemed to effortlessly handle those brutes last night and had been kind enough to take care of her.*

She gazed at the clean bandages wrapped around her forearm. She, in her groggy panic, hadn't even noticed it until now. Her fingertips grazed over the bandages as a thin smile slid across her face. That made her mind for her. She was going to get to know Dillon whether he liked it or not. A decision with ramifications far beyond either of their imaginations.

"How do you like your eggs?" Dillon asks as Liz emerges from the hallway, guided by the enticing aroma of bacon.

"Scrambled, I can never make it any other way." She shyly giggles. Liz is hoping he can't tell how forced the laugh is on her part as she is desperately clinging to any normal conversation she can. Some part of her is convinced that if they can imitate the normal mediocracy which most people lived then the nightmares from last night would just be nightmares.

She comes up and sits at the countertop as he cooks. She immediately looks down after she hops in the chair and realizes her feet don't touch the ground. Her legs begin gently kicking back and forth in an absent-minded manor as would any child. She sees two glasses of water and two of orange juice next to her.

"Are these for us?" she inquires, failing to stir up small talk as he simply nods to affirm her question. His head is down as he focuses on the food he is cooking, causing him to miss the discouraged look on her face. His demeanor has become somewhat guarded since he first unlocked her door, she realizes. Sheepishly sipping her glass of juice, she takes in the lavish apartment for the first time. It's impressive, and expensive. From how high up they currently are she guesses it's a penthouse. It seems to be a nice building, at least if they are all this nice. All the furniture looks high end, although she cannot figure out why the couch looks so filthy if everything else looks so pristine.

What does he do? She wonders. He clearly is not in dire need of cash by the looks of his apartment. The moment she asks herself that question her mind begins spiraling with all the possibilities. She begins paying closer attention to everything she sees, trying to play detective and solve the mystery that is Dillon. She remembers how he had handled himself far too well with those thugs from last night, meaning he was no stranger to fighting. That means he is no regular white-collar pencil pusher. Any possibility of him being some worker bee sipping coffee in his cubicle could be ruled out just by looking at the man. She is suddenly happy that he isn't paying her any attention as she soaks up everything detail about him. The only hints of his age are the few gray hairs rising out of his hair and scruff, the laugh lines around his eyes and mouth, and the leathery golden sheen to his skin which pointed towards hundreds of thousands of hours out in the sun. His tanned hide was tightly wrapped around his muscles which were subtle yet large at the same time, like a construction worker or a farmer who has been doing the same physically demanding job for years. His clothes are just loose enough to conceal how defined he is.

"What do you do? Like for work." She asks. "Sorry, what *did* you do?" She fumbles to recover from her verbal stumble. Liz is initially discouraged when at first, he seems not to hear her. Seconds tick by so slow as she awaits a response, each moment stretching into minutes.

"I *do* as little as humanly possible." He replies flatly, not intending to bring the subtle smile to her face that he does. It is so painfully obvious how hard he is trying to avoid the subject. "I occasionally teach tourist to sail. But I haven't taught anyone in well over a month." He added without ever looking up, displaying almost no interest in the conversation.

Apocalypse Virus: Initial Infection

"What did you do before that?" She presses further, "Like what kind of job is so cushy that you can afford a sweet pad like this in Tampa? So close to the water and yet you still hardly work?"

Her eagerness betrays her attempts to sound cool and casual.

"Let's talk about something else." He groans trying to make it seem like he is bored with the conversation. It comes out more agitated than anything else. She can, however, tell that there is something about the subject that he just doesn't want to talk about. Every sentence makes her ever more perplexed by her savior. "Where are you from Liz?" He asks to take hold of the reigns and steer this conversation back to what he deems as a safe or safer topic.

"Well I am from…" Dillon freezes as she trails off. A statue of an animal awaiting discovery. "wait, are you cooking on a camping stove?" she says confused as she peers over the counter blocking her view of the pan. He begins to laugh a little bit as it registers why she seems so confused. Relief floods over him as he realizes she has no clue as to why he is on edge. "Why the hell are you using that instead of the stove?" An incredulously toned squeak burst out of her as she asks her question.

"Building power is still out, which is also why I'm trying to cook all the cold goods before they go bad." He gestured towards the fridge. "I have some solar panels I normally use for camping laid out on the balcony charging so that we can microwave some of the frozen shit later. Hope you're hungry!" he says as a simplistic grin consumes his face, like one of those cartoon characters who you were never sure whether their eyes were open or closed. She sits there, mouth open, in wonder of how not only his way of thinking but also how he seems to take everything in stride as easy as if this were a common occurrence.

She starts to say something but decides against it. So, the two of them sit there the remainder of the morning eating and making small talk. Yet after a few hours Liz feels as though she is no closer to understanding him or getting to know him than she had been when she had first awoken this morning.

Around the middle of the day Dillon sets up an old radio. A relic of simpler times that his mom and dad used to use when the family would be huddled in the bathroom or playing board games under the candlelight during bad storms. A frequent occurrence over the years growing up in Florida. It picked up the emergency broadcast signals that the government puts out during natural disasters. It had gotten so hard for him to find batteries after they stopped making them about ten years back. At first, he had created a battery charger to try and make the batteries last longer, but it didn't really help. The batteries would make it maybe a half a dozen recharges before dying completely or the one or two that exploded a little. Eventually he made a little insert that goes into the battery space that can either be charged beforehand to act kind of like the old batteries on power tools. It could also be plugged directly into any socket or USB port in case you forgot to charge it. He has it plugged into the solar panels right now. Just another shining example of his ingenuity and craftsmanship, even if some of the things he made or modified looked Frankenstein-ish.

The two of them can hear commotion coming from the streets all day. They do not leave the apartment all day aside from Dillon going to help and check on the occupants of the Lyon Apartment building and his hour guard duty at the front door. Throughout the Q&A, that Liz insist on most of the day, Dillon has learned only a little bit of valuable information about her. Despite how young and gorgeous he thinks she looks, she is 36, only three years younger than he is. She was a nurse from some small New England town and had come down on a vacation to meet up with her cousin. Dillon still doesn't understand why tourist flocked to his home state as much as they did.

Other than that, he keeps the conversation on trivial stuff to avoid divulging to much about himself. He has managed to keep his service a secret so far, although she is having a hard time believing his was simply a part time sailing instructor.

It is better this way though. Or so Dillon tells himself. Once again mentally reciting an old mantra from when he was younger. Emotions make things messy. That much was always true in the regular old craziness of the world, but it is a thousand times more accurate in this new insanity that they all had been thrown into. This helped to further justify his lifelong mentality of his own self isolation.

The course of the next day or so seems to march along to pretty much the same beat as today. Main difference is that Liz stopped freaking out when she first wakes up in the morning. The commotion from outside which heralds the impending chaos comes and goes just as fast. It's amazing how things calm down when the outside temperatures hit the 90's. The building is mostly peaceful. A few old neighborly grudges flare up with the craziness of everything being as messed up as it is.

Everyone is beginning to look to Dillon for answers more and more often than he would prefer. He also teaches them how to turn a lot of the house old items into weapons for them to use on guard duty. He isn't about to give up his personal weapons if he can help it. He has begun moving a lot of his stuff into his tank of an SUV. She is his little baby. Only used for weekend trips into the Everglades. It is an old black Escalade he had bought in his early twenties. She is still in peak performance after all this time. She has a 3-inch lift, tinted windows, mostly bullet proof, a brush guard, a wench, and the engine had been remodeled for a snorkel.

A cargo rack is on top and the best sound system he had been able to find. He has had to convert the fuel system to a hybrid of hydro and electric power after the oil crisis of 2021.

Dillon gathers a few of the stronger and more capable men and women throughout the apartment to help and fortified the entrances to help protect the residents. Over the course of several days various residents approach him panic stricken, looking for someone to put their minds at ease. He manages to put some long-lost acting skills to the test and pull them up from their personal doom and gloom back into the very real doom and gloom of this new hellish nightmare rising up around them.

He still feels uncomfortable talking to people about emotions and such, regardless of how old he has gotten. It is always jaded with a ridiculous amount of guess work. Each encounter leaves him more exhausted than the last. The social anxiety is ever so gradually bottling up into a tightly packed powder keg waiting to be ignited. Despite this internal turmoil he knows that he can never show any weakness like this. Everyone needs him now and he hated that more than the end of the world itself. He begins longing for conflict again on the third or fourth day after the End. The old familiar itch to lash out at anything and everything in his path. By the end of the sixth day he becomes concerned with the growing possibility of him lashing out on these still good people. This too only increases the burden pressing down on his broad shoulders. He has not trained any of them on combat, hoping they won't need it. Trying to prolong their lives in the light before an inevitable downfall into the abyss. Something which may prove fatal for them in the long run. How long can he keep back the floodwaters with sandbags and buckets as the water levels rise faster than he can clear it? A clock slowly ticks away. Counting down piece by piece until it will all fall apart again. The hands of time chasing him still, ever further past the apocalypse. He dares not stop or else it will all come back to him at once and consume him once again, this time maybe forever.

Chapter 6

Tampa, Florida

Dillon

One Week after things went to hell.

Dillon holds his eyes shut tight while he is attempting to hear himself think. The noise in the room is thunderous. Dillon is reminded of how he felt in the high school lunchroom, drowning in a sea of disgruntled voices trying to talk over the other. Continually increasing the volume of the counterproductive clamor. Dillon opens his eyes and stops massaging his temples as he stands up to address the noisy constituency of the Lyon building residents gathered in the building's dingy basement. Seriously, this basement doesn't look like it has been cleaned in all the years the building has been around. People are periodically squealing over rats and spiders.

"Be quiet!" he booms, silencing everyone. His deep raspy voice cutting across the room. The assembly of people stares at him in surprise and some with irritation. Many of them recognize Dillon, although some have the unspoken question of "*Who is this asshole?"* plastered across their faces. A man from the first floor Dillon doesn't recognize turns his back on Dillon and starts to talk again almost as quickly as he had stopped.

"That is enough!" Dillon says flatly, cutting off the man. More authority and aggression slipping into these three little words. An unspoken threat felt by his tone sending shivers down the spines of all in the room. The previously defiant man sits down very dejectedly. Everyone is now sitting closer to the edge of their seats, or rather they would be if not for the fact that most of them are standing. Everyone's eyes are just a bit wider than a moment before. The tension in the air is almost palpable. It has suddenly become clear who is likely to take charge to everyone in the room.

"Look, I know we are running low on food and supply. I recognize you all have people in the city you want to check on. Some of you even want to try and leave the city to find your loved ones but we need to keep the building safe. It is too dangerous out there right now." The room once again erupts into a clamor as people begin arguing all at once over what they should do. This time it takes Dillon a considerably greater time to settle the room. He has to think through plans and back up plans with lightning speed.

"All those who want to leave feel free to pack up your belongings and take you vehicle, but I would highly advise against it. The big streets and interstate are probably littered with abandoned cars and full of awful people trying to take advantage of good-hearted individuals like yourselves. They are waiting to ambush good people like yourselves. Those of you who want to check on others elsewhere in the city I ask you to be patient and wait until we have successfully gathered up more supplies before you leave. If you help with getting more supplies I promise, we will help you look for your people. We must act and think as a group if we are to stay safe. Can everyone accept that?"

All nod, some clearly more reluctant or skeptical than the rest.

"Alright, with that settled can I get you," He says turning to Frank the doorman, "to go around the building and get a head count for how many want to leave and how many want to find people in the city so we can better organize ourselves?"

"No Problem. I know everyone in the building by this point so it shouldn't take long." Frank replies, grinning back at him. The young doorman is a sight to look at. He had been given some clothes by some of the other men since his doorman's uniform was the only clothing he had at the building when everything had happened. He now wears some slightly baggy bleach splattered jeans he had gotten from Bobby, and a now sleeveless flannel he got from someone else.

"Sweet. Alright for supplies I think five person squads would be best. Small enough to hide and be fast but large enough to stand a good chance if they run into trouble. A team lead will be elected by people not in the group and that person will be given a radio. I have a transmission set I can set up at Franks desk where someone can monitor the groups status and try to direct them with some maps of the city. We will have at max two teams out at the same time. And I want to make sure everyone who goes on these runs has some basic first aid skills in case things get messy out there so we will have a sign up for anyone who wants to go on a run at the front desk for the next day. It will be picked up at noon tomorrow and I will give those people a basic first aid course. We can make weapons for you if you want them. Anyone who wants to leave for good, or at least for the foreseeable future can leave tonight to make it so we don't have to bring in as much supplies. Any bitches, gripes, or complaints?" He inquires in conclusion to his monologue.

Kirtland D. Neal

The silence which follows implies that either all agreed, or they were all just tired of the rough man.

"Well if there aren't any issues with the game plan, I just outlined then I'll assume that everyone hear is good with that plan." He is answered with more silence. He begins to walk away from his section of the room and everyone else instinctively takes this as the cue to leave as well. He is pushing past people who quickly make way for this mountain of man as he makes his way back towards his apartment, Liz trailing at his coat tails. The image is akin to a younger sibling shadowing the older brother. She is more mystified by him every moment she spends with him as he becomes more complex and leaving her with more questions than answers. She finds it down right maddening. Much like a wildlife expert studying the behaviors of an animal they do not exactly understand regardless of the research the performed.

Liz is getting frustrated. A little bit with Dillon for being such a closed off mystery. However, she knows that is not what has her so irate. She is angry with herself. Liz is hit with that feeling of inadequacy as she silently follows Dillon back upstairs. In the last seven days she has not been able to do anything of value. She was helpless on the streets when he found her. She burned the food the one-time Dillon let her cook. He still ate it and smiled to try and make her feel better, but she found herself crying about it later when he was out of the apartment. She was barely able to help with the guard duties. She couldn't even give new knowledge on taking care of the sick and injured because it appeared as though Dillon knew it all, as though he might have been a doctor once upon a time. She has no idea how she might prove her value to this monument of a man. *How was he so calm and capable when facing such insane times?* Questions like this seemed to plague her thoughts more frequently as the days passed.

Apocalypse Virus: Initial Infection

As she walks up those thousands of stairs she is suddenly back in her hometown. She is once again that small child getting made fun of and running from a bully. She feels as helpless as the day she lost her sister, Jessie. Her mind is flooded with frightening memories. Her heart aches as these troublesome memories bubble up to the surface. It is taking everything she has now just to refrain from crying.

Liz is in such a daze that she doesn't realize Dillon has stopped until she runs straight into his back. She starts to feel herself fall backwards. Her eyes close and a scream escapes her lips as she expects to fall down a few flights of stairs before she stops falling. Her eyes flash open right as it happens. He spins around and is somehow right beneath her and catching her. He moves faster than she has ever seen someone move. Everything about him seems superhuman to her.

"You alright there?" Dillon asks her nonchalantly as she looks up into his eyes. *God his eyes*. Liz hadn't realized until this moment just how blue and beautiful his eyes are with a starburst of stormy gray in them which reminded her of the stormy sea. She is gazing up into his eyes and realizing for the first time just how ruggedly handsome this man is. She is absolutely transfixed by his eyes. "Liz?" She is snapped out her haze for a second.

"I am much better now." She says in a far-off voice, one which seems to come from someone else. Her hand moves up to his face and caresses his cheek. His face turns a light crimson. Dillon goes to stand her up. He gently removes her hand from his face and turns away. She is still mesmerized when he exits the last door before the roof and begins to go down the hallway which he has stopped at.

"You coming?" He calls over his shoulder without looking back after he doesn't hear her footsteps behind him. She is shaken out of her stupor and hurries to catch up.

"Dammit. That was close". Dillon tells himself, *"You almost kissed her. What were you thinking you jackass? Do not get emotionally involved. If you get involved, she becomes a liability and then you both die. You cannot die because you are protecting someone else! Hell, even if it weren't life or death you know she is still better off not getting attached to you like that."* he finishes his self-chastisement by the time they get back to the apartment.

His hands automatically fumble the keys into the locked door before pushing it open.

It is still early morning, yet Dillon feels like he's already had a long day. He leaves the door cracked open for his new shadow to come in through once she catches up. He walks in the master bathroom, habitually locking the bedroom door behind him. He stares at himself in the mirror, hands gripping the sink on either side. He stares at the reflection in much the same way he has stared at himself most of his life. A darker part of him taking over his thoughts as he delves into that brief period of what he fondly calls insanity. His oldest friend at this point in his life. No, friend is the wrong word, companion seems a better fit. He starts to question himself.

"Who are you to take charge? You're not special in the least bit. How dare you lead these people! These people will die because you are too weak and useless to save yourself, let alone anyone else. You are as worthless as you have always been! You are just strong enough to avoid death, yet continue on, too weak to ever truly live. Too much of a coward to end it anymore no matter how much you want too." Tears begin to silently cascade down his face as his fights with himself again. His mouth widens as much as it is physically capable in an inaudible scream which only, he can hear in his head. It is deafening. He feels the weight

of the world crushing him, pressing in on him at every angle. A diver being crushed by the pressure of the stygian depths of his ocean of self-hatred. His hands go back and forth from holding on to the vanity top and holding the sides of his head to try and keep the craziness and pain inside. He pulls on his hair, almost ripping it from his skull.

This is a fight he has been through countless times. The waring of good and bad wages inside of him so violently it inhibits him from doing anything else but to endure this storm. A storm which most commonly occurs in the late hours of the night after everyone else has gone to bed. When he is the only one up to face his demons.

"Admit it you bastard! You enjoyed being able to let loose and hurt those people like you did a few days ago. You need the rush of the fight. You are good for nothing else but to cause and endure violence. A glorified punching bag. You hope one of them is strong enough to do what you were too weak to do so many years ago. You want them to be stronger! You don't want to win! You pray for the day when you find the one who is strong or clever enough to kill you, your miserable wretch of a man. You are a cowardly murderer." He is in agony as all his body tenses and tightens up worse than any other moment besides these struggles.

"No! You are wrong!" he tells the darkness inside of him, *"I am strong enough to lead them. I do enjoy the rush of the fight, but I am not weak. I am strong. Strong enough to survive. Great enough to outlast everyone. I am willing to take on everyone's pain and torment because I know that I can bear the weight of it and more. It is the fuel that pushes me further! You are nothing! Nothing but the insecurities and darkness I have lifted off others and taken into myself. I am everything! I can do anything!"* he is deaf to all else as he yells at himself. He eventually ends up in a

ball on the cold tile floor as time passes by. This whole time he never even makes a sound. This debate wages on for close to an hour.

Later that evening the lobby is packed with people. Neighbors saying goodbye to each other for what may very well be the last time. Dillon is surprised by the number of people leaving. Almost the entire building plans to leave. They plan on going in a group and then peeling off as they get closer to their destinations. Dillon is positive they are all going to die within the next 48 hours, yet he respects their decisions to leave, hoping they surpass his expectations. Dillon turns as he finishes saying goodbye to Benny Vitelli just in time to see Frank rushing up to him.

"What's up Frank?" he asks the flustered doorman.

"Hey D, um you got a sec?" Frank is answered with a nod. "Great, well not great exactly. Umm…. We might have a problem. You remember how you asked me to do that head count you asked for? And I said I could handle it no problem since I know everyone in the building and what not. Well I did it and only about 20 or so people plan to stay according to my count. We won't have enough people to have lookouts all day and night. What are we going to do?" Frank asks, the young man getting ever twitchier and more nervous. Dillon groans as he rubs his face.

"God this fucking sucks, this sucks so damn hard." Dillon says as he grabs the back of his neck looking up at the ceiling as he gets increasingly stressed. Desperately trying to concoct some new plan which doesn't result in all of them dying. "We will…. We will just have to wait until the morning and see how many of the people actually stay behind." He says the anxiety in his voice incredibly audible. The anxiety almost drowns out his usually stoic and forced optimism. Frank is getting to see Dillon display his real emotions for the second or third time in the entire year or so that they've known each other. It is disconcerting to Frank to see his friend this way. Frank is worrying more and more as this conversation progressed.

"I am going back up to my place. Have someone come and get me if anything crazy happens while I am sleeping." Dillon finishes as he turns for the stairs, "Night Frank, look after the place for me will you." He sounds like himself again as he speaks so casually.

"Everything is going to be fine. Don't you go worrying yourself." He finishes as he squeezes Frank's shoulder when he brushes past.

Dillon is hit with wave of cold shock as he splashes water on his face and looks at himself in the mirror. Staring hard into those blood shot eyes. The face staring back at him seems like it belonged to a stranger. The decent little beard he had managed to grow in the last few days only made him appear as an entirely different man than the one who he had become accustomed to seeing across the dirty mirror. He is scared to acknowledge this haunting reflection as his new self. He stands there wondering what happened to the young, hopeful, twenty something year old version of himself who was so ambitious, had so many dreams. What had led that same kid down the path to this skeptical, angry man of almost 40 years who felt more alive in the heat of a fight or giving orders to others, regardless of how stressful it might be to make those calls.

He is so lost in thought and self-contemplation he doesn't notice Liz watching him from the doorway until she reaches out a hesitant hand gently grabs him on the shoulder. Her surprising touch is enough to startle him out of his daze and he turns to face her incredibly fast. He grips her outstretched arm by the wrist. The dark look in his eyes sends a rush of fear through her. A moment or two later and he releases her hand, the look in his eyes giving way to the normally controlled and gentler look he normally wears.

"I am sorry I shouldn't have snuck up on you like that." Liz says as she turns away and makes a hasty retreat to her room which he has so kindly let her stay in. She immediately regrets disturbing him. He simply frowns down at the ground. Upset with himself for turning on her like that, even if accidentally. Despite this he is too worn out after the long day he has experienced to chase her down and express his remorse. Feeling slightly self-defeated he simply goes to bed. He can't remember how many hours it has been since last he ate. He's too fatigued to worry about food now. He isn't settled under the covers more than a few minutes before he drifts off into sleep.

Dillon is stirred from his sleep by someone vigorously shaking him. His hand shoots out and grabs the hand shaking him so fast the person yelps like an injured pup. He opens his eyes to find it was Liz who was doing the shaking and Frank is peering warily over her shoulder. They both hold the looks of small children who had woken their parents for something a silly as a bad dream and were starting to think they might be yelled at. A pair of deer poking a sleeping grizzly bear. Releasing her hand, Dillon closes his eyes and rolls back over. Neither Liz nor Frank says anything for a few moments. Not sure what to make of his actions. Dillon can hear their hesitation and uncertainty

"What do you want?" he asks ever so groggily over his shoulder, "What could not wait until the morning?" a tone of irritation sliding in there. The two whisper as though neither wanted to tell him what they woke him for. After a few minutes of their hushed bickering he turns over towards them and stares at them with such grouchiness and perplexity. "Dammit! Will one of you spit it out already!" His voice croaking loudly, still dry from the deep slumber he had been in. He is now propped up on his elbows, the covers falling low enough to reveal his shirtless chest.

Apocalypse Virus: Initial Infection
"There's practically no one left D." Frank says,
unable to bring his eyes up from the floor to meet Dillon's eyes.

"It is alright Franky. We don't hold people here against
their will. If they want to risk their lives for an attempt at freedom,
then let them." D says, more softly than he had spoken in the
several days since this hell came to them. A hand reaches up to
pat the young man on the head in reassurance. Liz thinks she sees
what is almost a soft and gentle expression sprawled across the
man's face. *Must be the dim lighting* she tells herself as images of
him rescuing her playback in high definition. "Both of you get out
really quick. I need to get dressed so I can deal with things before
they get worse." They close the door and Dillon groans as he sees
it is barely two in the morning. He swings his legs over the side of
the bed and proceeds to get dressed in the dark. He has no trouble
seeing through the hues of black and gray. He never has.

The music begins blaring as soon as the door is closed.
This morning's soundtrack is one resembling the raves Liz
remembered her and her sorority used to go to. Steve Aoki is the
first one up to bat today. She is barely able to remember anything
from those concerts besides the actual music itself. She was
usually high on either X or some psychedelics. Admittedly some
of the best years of her life, even if they were a bit of a haze.

Dillon's mind is racing as he throws an old tank top over
his head. This one is an old Captain America one, almost faded
beyond recognition. His go-to work out shirt. The electronic
music is helping to make all neurons fire in overdrive first thing in
the morning. The red bull he pounds back from his mini fridge
helps spark that fire, but what does that matter? Well, that and the
line of cocaine he snorts. More like rocket fuel than gas on the
fire. *First things first,* he thinks as he pulls his jeans up and laces
up the old black boots he likes so much, *I need to get everything*

that's left in the apartment packed and in the Tank. Walking fast he leaves his room, crossing the 20 or 30 feet to the kitchen in seconds as the others trail behind him. With their shoulders suddenly perking up now, in much the same way a pack stands tall as an alpha shows a glimmer of its prowess. A previously unnoticed weight seems to be removed from their shoulders, the two exit the hallway outside the dark bedroom.

The two of them are more shocked than anything when they look up to see him with a kindhearted smile on his face, his eyes halfway shut. *Okay, so maybe it isn't just the darkness that made him look…comforting.* Liz debates internally. Dee resembles a father making his best effort to reassure uncertain children.

"Alright Frank." He addresses the young man without even looking back. "What around here went to shit while I was sleeping this time?" Dillon asks as he starts the coffee pot. There is more irritation in his voice than he means too. He had done a less than visually appealing job when he had hotwired the coffee maker into a smaller solar panel and battery the first morning after the proverbial shit hit the fan. The two take turns giving Dillon the breakdown as the coffee brews and are finished by the time he finishes his first cup. Straight black, just like momma always drank it.

"So long story short, all that's left is us three, the stoner twins next door, Kate and her boy from downstairs, and Ali and her dog, Brutus. The rest have left and now there is nowhere near enough people to maintain control of this building. Oh, and the degenerates that use to be decent people are increasing in numbers on the streets to make things worse. That about sum up how royally screwed we are?" He asks between sips of his coffee. They both nod worried looks coming over them both. Dillon is as calm as ever. Unflinching. Calculating.

"Alright. Go tell the others to pack their things and meet me in the lobby if they wish to come with us." He drank another mouthful of piping hot coffee before stopping them to add, "Tell them they have, let's say two, no, no. Let's make it three hours. We roll out just after 0530." He waves at them to leave this time. He finishes his second cup and pours a third as he sits down on the couch contemplating how insane his plan makes him. Would the others even go with him? Do they even want to or are they just trying to stay alive? Should they? The plan he was cooking up was very mad. Not just mad but certifiable as far as he was concerned.

He begins to look around the place which he has come to call home over the last year or so after he moved into his former vacation home. There are so many memories in this place. He isn't ready to deal with this level of nostalgia this early. Or without any alcohol for that matter. He has a creeping suspicion that this new, harsher, more chaotic world would seldom allow for moments of peaceful nostalgia. Shaking off the feelings he feel coming he begins to get lost in work as he starts to move around the loft and finishes packing up anything he doesn't want to leave behind. He makes sure to grab all the drives with the thousands of hours of music he had illegally downloaded over the years. Some he even got from Livewire when he was barely a teenager back when everything was burned to either floppy disc or CD's.

He finishes his second pot of coffee and is packing that up as the last thing he has to pack when the other two had returned. Frank isn't paying as much attention as Liz and trips over one of the totes as he comes in the door. The tote was fine but Frank was a different story. The guy went tumbling right into the wall leaving a sizeable hole in the wall. The crash caused one of Dillon's massive speakers to fall above Frank. Once again Liz is astounded by how fast Dillon can move. He seems to cover the distance between the balcony and Frank in a single moment. Just in time to catch the speaker before it can crush Frank.

"Got to be more careful dude." Dillon says while he walks the rather large speaker over to the couch. Liz can't help but to notice how amazing his back muscles looked as he carried the speaker away. This is the first time she has seen him with this much of his back shown, she is not the least bit disappointed. Her imagination begins to drift to images of him and her in a manner that surprises Liz herself for even thinking these thoughts. Despite his age, Dillon has the body of someone in his twenties, well with a great deal more pain than what a younger him had felt. A body which reflects the countless hours he spends in the gym each week, an obsessive habit he got at the end of high school. Liz doesn't realize how long she had been staring, transfixed by this man, until Frank is waving his hand in front of her face giggling. Her gaze drops to the floor as her cheeks turn a deep red. Frank's pleasure is cut short when her hand shoots out and hits him in the gut.

Dillon is confused why Frank is holding his stomach and Liz is red faced glaring at the ground when he turns around from putting the speaker down. Shaking his head, he resumes packing up the last box.

"You two losers talk to everyone left?" He glances out the corner of his eye to see them nodding, "So are they all coming with us?" He looks up after a moment or two of silence to see Frank staring at the ground like a child afraid to tell his parent what he had done wrong. Liz is no better, she is anxiously biting her lip and staring at a random spot on the wall. "What is it?" he asks, his voice gaining a degree of rigidness and dominance.

"None of them want to come. They all said they aren't going to leave with us like they weren't going to leave with the others. Or at least in some form another they said that." Says

Frank, bringing his gaze up slightly yet still averting eye contact with Dillon.

"Fine. Let them die here if they want." Dillon says as he closed the final box shrugging off what they had just told him. The two no longer avoid eye contact as their eyes shoot up to stare at Dillon in amazement, neither is able to believe what he has just said. "Liz, I found a set of my ex's clothes I never threw out after she moved out while finding stuff, it's in there on your bed." Dillon walks over to the bar top and pulled his shirt down over his head. "Frank, one of my friends was about your size and left some of his clothes here after his visit last week. It should be in the bathroom." The two are so far beyond stunned from his initial response that they can't move. Dillon picks up one of the boxes and starts to carry it to the truck before he realizes they might as well have been stone figures in that moment. Setting down the box he casually walks over to them, straightening out his shirt. Without any warning he proceeds to slap both of them out of their stupor. It makes a rather satisfying noise as his hands connect to their faces. Both appear equally hurt, which he is completely oblivious to.

"There we are!" he says with a smile, arms outstretched, as they both seem to have snapped out of their haze. He is proud of himself as though he had done them a favor. "Now if you two are ready I managed to find some clothes I think will fit y'all, they're in the guest bedroom and bathroom. So, go get dressed and then we can pack the last of this shit in my car before we head out." They both seem to agree, although they are still evidently sour about him slapping them. They would soon forget about it. Dillon knows that the last week would soon be forgotten as he remembered what he had been seeing through his binoculars the last few days. The shadowy figures he refused to tell the others about. Him slapping them would seem gentle to them before the day was over.

Kirtland D. Neal

Dillon had sent the other two to say their final goodbyes to everyone. He begins to think about all that he could have done differently in his life up until this point. He mulls this train of thought over as he gets dressed for real. Reviewing every decision, he had made and thinking about the possible consequences, like some elaborate chess game, predicting moves. As he straps the last knife in, he realizes he wouldn't have done it any differently, a smile slowly spreading across his face. Dillon throws his old deployment bag over his back after clipping the 12 gauge to his back. He grabs his AR as he starts to walk out of his room, armed to the teeth. Stopping just in the doorway he turns to the room one last time before closing the door. He double checks the entire loft for anything he might have overlooked. The only thing to make the somber occasion of the final walk through of his home somewhat delightful was that he is welcomed by one his favorite spectacles. The rising sun's fingers of light seemed to grip every room in embrace, as though she too was saying goodbye to this place forever. He loved the morning glow of this place. He look out on the bay from up here one final time.

Frank and Liz stop as they turn out the stairwell and see Dillon leaving the loft. He, in their eyes, resembled some modern-day version of a demigod of war, or at least a bad ass looking soldier. He has two pistols holstered under both armpits. There was a third pistol on his right thigh, a tomahawk on the opposite thigh. The end of a double barrel shotgun peered from behind him. And some sort of assault rifle in his hands. He has on camo cargo pants, every pocket seemed to be filled to the max, the pants come down and are tucked into some coyote brown steel toed boots. He has a simple black shirt with an odd-looking vest over it now. He had a decent sixed camo bag across his back. A backwards baseball cap on his head, a pair of top shelf sunglasses pushed up on them. Black gloves on his hands and bandanas tied around each wrist.

"Why…uh...why are you dressed like that?" Frank asks as his voice trembles.

"Let's pray we don't have to find out." He says as he walked pass them into the stair well. "Come on! It's time to go play soldiers in a Humvee." He calls over his shoulder with an unsettling smile and odd amount of cheer.

Chapter 7

Somewhere in Southern Florida

Tabitha

October 25, 2029

It has been roughly two months since the break in at the lab. All their data had been taken along with all of Tabitha's work from the previous few months. To make matters worse the lab had also been vandalized and torched. The built-in sprinklers kept it from burning to the ground, but everything was ruined from either smoke, fire, or water damage. Which made it even harder to tell what was taken and what was simply destroyed. The authorities were never notified due to the, well the classified nature of their work. So instead STS sent a team of their own investigators from the company's private security firm, the Black Ravens. After a few weeks of interrogations, the team ruled out anyone from the lab, thus allowing them to restart all their research. The Ravens are now more present than she had ever seen them.

Tabitha is unsure what to think of the renovations as she walks into the lab for the first time since it had gotten robbed and burnt. Much of the facility is still under reconstruction but there was enough of it restored for everyday operations to start back up.

Apocalypse Virus: Initial Infection

The renovations that are completed already made the old set up, which was revolutionary, look old and outdated.

The security protocols are now even worse than any airport. They are not allowed to bring in any personal devices such as phones, laptops, tablets, etc. And there is now an x-ray machine they have to walk through while some Raven looks over everything that shows up. The once subtle front area had gone from a warm charcoal gray that made it seem like it could have been a hotel lobby, and now had risen ceilings, all shiny metal fixtures and marble floors and walls. It looks like the big fancy STS buildings that they advertised all the time. There is something cold and clinical to it now.

The food court is almost too much for Tabitha to handle. It is larger and more diverse than any mall or airport food court that she had ever seen. She had been to the Mall of America. She is slowly wandering around in awe, like a child at an amusement park. The escalator that carries her upstairs to the labs now has a massive LED screen above it which plays various company stuff on a loop. Promotion videos, company messages reminding people on proper protocol and professional etiquette. The lab and various other rooms that she ventures through the rest of the day are just as grand as what she had seen downstairs.

It takes Tabitha roughly two weeks before she ceases wandering the facility in a constant state of wonder. Now it is back to being just work. A week ago, she had begun to notice that some of her fellow employees have started to disappear, gotten transferred, or just began to act differently all together. Ricco was amongst them. There was no real clear reason why they were disappearing or acting different, but not wanting to cause a fuss she just lets things persist without any outcry from her. No one else seems to notice it or at least if they did, they didn't share this concern with Tabitha. For the most part keeping calm was easy.

The only hard part is working beside the once over-talkative and extremely hyper Ricco who might as well be a mute now the way he acts around her. They no longer have their usual banter or enjoy lunch together. It is almost as though he is trying to avoid her.

Today is November 19th. A Monday. Tabitha is walking into the lab about 15 minutes earlier than she normally does, trying to put in some extra hours before the holiday week. She stops dead in her tracks as she rounds the corner, almost snapping one stiletto in half in the process. Her ankle even does the wobble thing that women's ankle sometimes do. She barely manages to avoid completely snapping off the heel. She retreats around the corner she just rounded and peers her head around the wall to make sure she is seeing what she thought she did. About 25 yards down the hall, right by the lab door, there stands three shadowy figures. The tallest one seems to exude command and demand respect, which is readily given by the other two. He is a tan man in a royal blue suit with a brown pea coat over top. An old looking brimmed hat on his crop of gelled brown hair. A rounded pair of glasses, which makes him look older, sit low on his nose and slightly crooked. A worn leather briefcase in one hand. *He almost looks like… no, there's no way.* She thinks to herself. *Is that Mr. McKenzie himself? Why would he ever need to be at some small, irrelevant research facility like this one?*

Mr. McKenzie, or James McKenzie, was the founder and CEO of Summerfield Technical Solutions. She had never seen him in person before, but his reputation for being a handsome man was not exaggerated in the lightest.

To Mr. McKenzie's left stands a light brown man not too much shorter than Mr. McKenzie, dressed in an all black military looking uniform that belongs to the Ravens. And other than the surface image she has no idea who he is or what he might be like. The third man is the most shocking of all to her. Ricco. There is no doubt about it in her mind, that is Ricco. The same guy she had worked so many countless hours within the last year or so. The immature, never serious Ricco is having a straight-faced conversation which seems serious based off the three men's expressions. There is a furrow to Ricco's face she has never seen before that makes him almost look like a completely different person, the opposite of the friend she had known.

She has to find a better place to listen in without being spotted. She slowly backs up and turns to double back around, utilizing one of the hallways she had passed. She has snuck into a small alcove in a wall just a few feet away from the end of the hallway the men stand by.

"Does she know anything about what really happened?" A man with a deep voice asks, somewhat hushed.

"From what I've gathered so far Mr. Alverez, she knows nothing about that night." Ricco addresses to Mr. Alverez, the Raven man she had seen. "Or at least if she does then she has yet to mention it me." He adds upon seeing the menacing furrow in the Raven's brow.

"Good. that makes her less of a liability then." Says a third voice, Mr. McKenzie she is assuming. "Argo, I want you to keep watching her and guiding her. Our plan must succeed. Now we will not be meeting like this in public again if we can avoid it, alright?" A brief pause passes before he resumes. "Remember we are the catalyst. And we are what will drive evolution ever forward." He almost shouts. The other two men repeating him.

She hears them separate in different directions. With a set of footsteps fast approaching she tries to press her body against the wall as much as she can, as if trying to will herself to merge into the wall. The footsteps become deafening as the person draws ever closer. The only thing she can hear over the steps is her heart, threatening to beat right out her chest. Tabitha feels like she is drowning in a sea of fear and panic. Clenching her eyes shut and holding one hand over her mouth too silence her breathing. The person is but a few feet away from where she is hidden. Her heart rate spikes with every step. She is playing every possible scenario she can think of right now, none of them good. In each one she ends up dead or worse.

Now the footsteps are right in front of her. She slowly opens her eyes, for what may very well be the last thing she ever sees. She grows rigid from shock, too surprised and terrified to even breath for a moment. It's Ricco. He seems to be adjusting something tucked into the back of his waist band. His lab coat furls up with his steps to reveal the glimmer of a dark metal handle. *A gun!* Tabitha is petrified, a paralysis onset by pure fear. Ricco keeps walking, never seeing her, too busy adjusting the gun he has tucked away.

And then what feels like an eternity passes before Tabitha no longer hears footsteps. She rushes forth from her concealment and makes a bee line for the restroom. She checks to make sure the room is empty before she locks the door. And now that she feels a moment of safety she collapses to the cold tiled floor. She begins to cry so violently, yet never allows herself to make a sound. She is there for a long time. Balling herself up and weeping on the filthy bathroom floor. Trying hard to come to terms with what she has seen and heard in the hallway.

Are they watching her? But why would they? What is so special about her? She can not even begin to answer these questions. Only one thing is certain, she is now in danger for simply having overheard the conversation. Though she does not know why or for what reason. She can't simply run, they would either find her or hurt her family. She has a strong feeling that she can't go to the authorities based off of how easily they concealed the break in. STS supplies most government agencies with state of the art equipment, including local law enforcement. She can only see one option to try and survive this. She must keep going about her business as usual, while trying to discern what terrible plot is in the works and make plans to escape should the need arise. One question bothers her above the rest.

Why were they so interested in her?

She quickly resolves herself to do the only thing she can see working out in her favor. She goes into work almost an hour early every day and stays an hour or so late every day. When others are with her, she works on the company research, working harder than she has worked on it previously. When she is alone however, she snoops around slowly uncovering scraps of information about what is really going on.

As of today, just three days before Christmas, she has not found any earth-shattering evidence of maliciousness. She shows up to work an hour early as has become customary for her the last month or so. She waves at Tony, the front guard in charge of the scanner as she walks through.

"Another early start, Tabi?" He asks her like he asked at least once a week.

"Is it wrong that I just can't wait to see you in the mornings Tony?" She catches his attention, sounding more flirtatious than normal. A low, seductive purr consuming her normal tone of voice.

"You keep coming in early just to see me and people might begin to wonder" He says with a wink, trying to awkwardly laugh it off. He is sure that a woman like her would never go for someone like him. "What am I supposed to tell my fiancé should she hear rumors like that?" he laughs.

"There nothing wrong with having a work wife Tony." She says carefully tracing his broad arm with the tips of her nails. His muscles give a small, yet visible quiver as she gets halfway up his arm. *Damn I'm good!* She thinks to herself as Tony seems to be drawn into her, his gaze never rises above her exceptionally low cropped blouse. The crimson red makes her fair complexion look even more appealing, or at least that's what her mother had often told her.

"Now if you play your cards right Tony, you might just get a closer, or shall I say more intimate view than your little scanner here." She runs her index and middle finger up his other arm, to the bottom of his collar bone and then up his neck to the bottom of his chin. Her fingers just barely gliding over his skin.

"Now how would you like that?" Her question is quickly affirmed by his rigorous nodding.

"Good!" she almost moans out as she grabs his tie and draws him ever nearer to her. She grabs the back of his neck, pulling him in the rest of the way for a passionate kiss. The kind of kiss that you can feel and taste on your lips for the rest of the day. She keeps the lip lock going for a minute or so before slowly breaking away and whispering in his ear.

"I will meet you in the security room after work, make sure no one else is there. Got it?" she asks with a seductive nibble of his ear as she pulls away a little. He nods, still stunned by what had happened.

Apocalypse Virus: Initial Infection

"Good. I will see you at five. Don't be late." She adds one last kiss before walking up to the lab. And just like that she has smuggled her things through the scanner. And hopefully her sensual performance would provide her with other benefits later. She walks through the labs, coffee in hand. Looking down at her watch she sees that it is still only 5:19. Not even the sun has risen yet. The other employees are as absent as the light of dawn. She has to move fast before the early birds show up. She grabs the blue box out of her purse, a device of her own making. She has taken the idea of how they duplicate the phones on television shows and movies. So now she has constructed this device, her own little Pandora's Box as it were, that is supposed to replicate all the data from any sort of computer or device she passes with in twenty feet of that is on. The Doppelganger as she has dubbed it.

Having turned it on and placing it back in her bag she casually walks through all the labs making sure to get close enough to the computers and the various servers. She tracks her progress with an app she had created on her phone. So, she appears to be playing on her phone and sipping her coffee while strolling through the labs. No cameras would be able to catch her doing anything suspicious. But to make sure she covered all her bases she is wearing a tech infused necklace that keeps the cameras from picking up her face, it is just a black and white pixelated blur where her head should be.

After walking through all the labs and computer rooms she makes her way to the sample storage room, where they kept all the samples and paper data. She had searched and collected as much data as she can for the morning. People have started to show up and sleepily resume wherever they had left off the day before. She goes into the restroom and removed her necklace and walks out. She goes to walk out the bathroom just to fumble into Ricco. She has enough time to spin around him before colliding into him. He looks up from some file he was reading, a bewildered look crossing his face.

"Sorry about that Ricco. I should be more careful when coming out of the ladies' room." She says in a friendly voice.

"You're fine." he replies in the same avoiding tone he has adopted after the break in.

They walk the rest of the way to the lab, carrying on the longest conversation they have had since the break in. He has been slowly warming back up to her ever since she had seen him and the other two talking in the hallway.

And that is the way the remainder of the day transpired. It is almost like it was before. But there is some unspoken chasm between them that they both sense but overlook. Five o'clock arrives slower than normal for Tabi. She rounds the corner to see a skittish looking Tony scanning the hallway relax and then perk up at the sight of her.

"I was beginning to think you weren't coming" he bleats out with a nervous grin. "Don't you worry about me not showing Tony," she coolly replies as she sensually walks toward him, putting an extra sway into her hips. "I was only ten minutes late. Now your only concern should be when you have me arriving." She utters with a wink as she throws her lips on his. He fumbles with the door while they make out. They barely slip into and lock the empty room by the time she has him pinned up against a wall in a passionate kiss and full body embrace. Before she knows it, their clothes have slid down to the floor. She makes sure to casually hit certain buttons as they fumbled around. Each pushing the other with animalistic intent. Tony picks her up and puts her on the control consul as his mouth kisses its way down her neck and over her collarbone until he eventually kisses his down to her lips. Meanwhile his hand travel where they wish, exploring as much of her as they can manage. She has to admit that even though this isn't her main objective that this is still an amazing idea. Before Tony knows it, she is mewling so loudly he thinks someone might hear them. Those fleeting concerns vanish the moment she pulls his shoulders up, silently commanding him to go for it.

With her hips balanced on top of his, Tony slams her against the wall a little harder than he means too. As he pushes and pulls her away from him, she rakes her nails over his back sending him ever higher into the euphoria of the situation. They have both arrived at their destination after a few dozen minutes of this passionate dance. Tony lowers them both on to their clothes. They both huff and puff as they struggle to catch their breath.

"Can you check my back and see how bad the scratches are?" Tony asks as he rolls over onto his stomach.

"Sure thing." She pounces on top of him, sitting on his butt. There is an aura of steam enveloping both of them at the moment. She takes this opportunity to kiss and massage him as she assesses the damage done. As she had hoped, he has a few spots where she had broken skin. This means that the sedative that she had laced her fingernails with should be taking effect any moment.

"There's maybe 3 or 4 spots where I broke skin but nothing major darling." She leans over to kiss the back of his head too find that he is already softly snoring. She quickly finds her purse and pulls out a small syringe with more of the same compound as had been in her nails. After removing the rubber plug stuck to the needle tip, she clears it of any air bubbles. She finds a good, meaty part of the mid-thigh, in what should be the Vastus Lateralis region. Once she is sure that she has found the right region she performs an intramuscular injection of the sedative. This helps ensure that he will be knocked out as long as she needs him to be.

Chapter 8

Tampa, Florida

January 11th, 2030

Eight days into hell.

By the time he is exiting the stairwell and crossing the now vacant lobby to the parking garage that connected to one side of the building Frank is overcome with a feeling that felt alien after the week and a half from hell. If he didn't know any better Frank might call it excitement. There is something about following Dillon, dressed ready to wage a one-man war on the world, and walking alongside Liz that fills him with confidence. It gives him the feeling that they will be alright despite what might happen as long as the three of them stay together.

Their footsteps ring out in an eerie echo as they jog through the parking lot to where Dillon's car is. Frank isn't sure what to expect Dillon's car to look like, but it definitely isn't what is parked a few levels up. The old black SUV looks it had been pimped out by some military outfit. The windows have bars to protect them and were seriously tinted. The tires are a few sizes bigger than what the vehicle should have on. It also has a solid 6-

inch lift if not more and the hub caps had these crazy looking spikes. There is a snorkel hugging the passenger side of the hood, just in front of the side mirror. Frank has never seen a snorkel on anything besides a jeep so that threw him off a bit. The grill is covered with a wicked looking brush guard that looks like it could split a building if it wanted to. There is what looks like a winch tucked away near the bottom of the brush guard. There is also a lot of stuff strapped to the roof of the little tank.

"Have you always had this here?" Frank asks as he stops and gawks at the SUV with Liz.

"Yes, normally has a cover over her unless I am working on her. Now are you going to keep staring at Lola or are you going to get in we can go?" Dillon says, sounding rushed as he climbs up behind the steering wheel. The two of them are shaken out of their wonder by the roar of the ignition as Lola springs to life. Liz and Frank have barely closed their doors before Dillon hits the gas and they race downwards to the street level.

"Wait a second. Weren't there more bodies out on the streets Dillon? I could have sworn that there were so many more bodies here that day you saved me." Liz asks with a tone of worry creeping up her throat as she talks. Nothing remaining but the blood stains, as though a distant reminder of an old event. Dillon won't meet her eyes but the look on his face says he knows more than he is willing to say, "What happened to the bodies Dillon?" Liz pressed a bit more.

"Don't ask things you don't want to know the answers to." He turns to tell her, the look on his face convinces her not to press the issue any further. She turns towards the window to gawk at the carnage left behind from the last week. The sense that no one is coming to help them seems to suffocate Liz.

Apocalypse Virus: Initial Infection

"What the hell is that?!" Frank asks from the back seat as he stares out the other side, eyeballing a passing alley way. The question shakes her from her worries, and she looks back only to catch a flash of something…something not exactly human. The way Dillon looks forward ever harder and purses his lips more tells them that he already knows the answer. What had he been doing when he was sneaking away the last week? She wonders to herself. What does he know that he isn't telling them?

They spend the next week or so snaking their way from building to building, each as seemingly random as the last to the two passengers. There is only one place they visit more than once. A private dock just a few blocks from Lyon Apartments. Dillon has them keep watch by the car while he ferries boxes of supplies to the enormous triple mast sailing yacht at the end of the dock. Liz is stunned to find out that Dillon has owned the ship for most of his adult life.

At the end of their second week in hell Dillon has decided everything is all set. He just needs to make one final stop before they set sail. They pull up to some old brick building with a now shattered neon light hanging by its side. Liz can barely make out one word: Pete's. The t is shattered leaving only a metal outline of the letter. The scene itself is hard to process. A group of several men are dragging three people out through a busted door. There is a man, easily as old as her and Dillon. Dillon can just make out enough of the man to know that it is in fact not Thad, but Ernie, the resident drunk who seems to live at the bar. He is wearing the same zig zag shirt he wears every day, the shirt reminds Dillon of a knock off Charlie Brown. A woman of about the same age, and a young female who barely looks old enough to be in high school are the other part of the trio to be dragged out. Dillon has a strong feeling that the two women are Thad's wife and daughter. He is left asking himself one question. Where is Thad? Dillon parks the car around the corner, just out of line of sight from the goons and victims. He quickly turns to the other two in the car.

Kirtland D. Neal

"Don't unlock these doors for anyone but me or those two women. Got it?" The tone in his voice makes it obvious this is more of a command than a request. He continues, cutting Liz off in what is undoubtedly some sort of protest to what he was about to do. "If you guys see me die then just drive to the marina. Once there hop on my boat and get the hell off the mainland for a while, maybe this shit hasn't spread to the islands. Head south through the bays and channels and try to shoot for one of the islands circled on the map."

Just like that the door is slamming shut and he is hurrying to his friends. Liz is still shocked, but she does as she is told and locks the doors. She is just hoping he was as indestructible as he acted. Even more mysteries about this seemingly impossible man begin spinning through her mind. There is a tense moment of silence.

"Why does he have a boat?" She turns back over the seat to look at Frank as she talks.

"He uses it to, or rather he used to use it to teach some of the more advanced sailors more professional sailing skills so they would have better chance at getting hired by some luxury sailing service, or their just rich pricks who wanted to learn to sail their oversized yacht's. It is also his personal one that he uses for trips and contest alike. He has shown me how to sail on it actually." Franks face twist into a faint smile as he remembers the enjoyable times they had shared on the boat. Their conversation is cut short as they hear a gunshot ring out across the previously silent street. They both crane their heads around to see the man in the zig zag shirt slam against the pavement, a cloud of red mist dissipating around him.

The closer he gets, the angrier Dillon grows. He has barely made it more than a few feet away from the truck when he sees Ernie get gunned down in front of the girls. Everyone in front of Pete's now has a light pinkish-red tint to them as the blood splatter settles over them. There are five men that he can count. Two of them are holding a crying Sonia who is trying to wiggle her way free. Another two are holding a defiant looking Jill. The fifth man tucks the pistol in his waist band just above his back-right pocket. He then turns to Jill and starts talking to her. The displeasure is written on her face as clear as if it were on a billboard.

Apparently, he said something which really pissed her off because her look of disgust turns to one of rage in the same second, she lunges forward. Her sudden movement catches her captors off guard allowing her to slip free of them long enough for her to bite the side of the gunner's face. Blood immediately begins pooling up from the wound. The two goons who had been holding her rush forward and pull her off the gunner. He is left holding his face as he uses a flurry of curse words, Dillon could only make out a few of the more colorful words as he closes the distance. As he is swearing, he reaches back with his free hand and back hands Jill hard enough to cause her head to spin all the way back to one side. Dillon speeds up his pace even more. His swelling pride for Jill's defiance is coupled with his growing concern that her and Sonia might receive the same fate as Ernie if he isn't fast enough.

The girls seem to perk up once they see Dillon. The men holding them seem to stiffen. Two of the four seemed hopeful for another fight. The one with the bite mark seems to feel the shift in attitude and turns to face Dillon head on now. *Son of a bitch!* Dillon thinks to himself. He knows who this dickhead is. His blood seems to boil even more with this realization.

"Is that really little ole Tommy Perez? Damn you must have grown up a lot if you have the balls to mess with Thad's family, especially since you didn't know if I was alive or not." Tommy turns to yell at one of his laughing lap dogs. The others don't seem to recognize who Dillon is.

"Dillon just keep walking along if you don't want any trouble. This don't concern you." Tommy's voice sounds tough and almost intimidating, but Dillon can sense some edginess to his voice. His eyes, however. His eyes are filled with pure unadulterated terror, darting all over, looking at everything but Dillon's eyes. The others are ignorant to how Tommy is on high alert since he has his back to them.

"You know I can't do that Tommy." Dillon says as he plays with the tomahawk in his hands, feigning disinterest. "Now why don't you just let Jill and Sonia come with me? Save me a lot of trouble and you boys a lot of ass pain. I'll even look past Ernie's death, I know he wasn't a saint. That said, even Ernie deserved better." Dillon gestures toward the corpses a few feet away, using the axe like a pointer. "I like to think he was just drinking until his liver ultimately shit out on him. So, what do you say, going to let the girls come with me?"

"I can't do that Dillon. It's not my choice." Tommy looks displeased to say no to Dillon, or is that fear? Dillon can't tell. Either way it looks as if his body wants to do what Dillon is asking but his mind is still forcing it to carry out the will of someone else. "We are doing as we are asked to, don't mean no harm by it."

"Tell that to Ernie, who is lying dead, still warm." Dillon says trying to be calm in the face of his overwhelming rage.

"Ernie, he just wasn't supposed to be in there. He refused to let things be, so I had to do something to keep him out our affairs."

Apocalypse Virus: Initial Infection

"Who's giving you orders Tommy?" He asks as he casually strolls closer to the group in an indirect and lackadaisical fashion to keep them from noticing that he is methodically closing the space between. Tommy flinches away from the question as if it might burn him. "Who is powerful enough to make you more afraid of them than me?" Silence hangs in the air for a few minutes as Dillon thinks about his own question. "Is it Alex, Alex Martinez?" The way the boy looks down to the ground confirms the question. Tommy doesn't have to say anything. He is as easy for Dillon to read as ever. "Alright man, alright. So, you're sure there's no way you can just let them go peacefully?" Tommy shakes his head with regret plastered on his face. A sea of emotions churns in the young man's chest. Dillon simply shrugs and changes trajectory. He is now making a bee line for the group now. There is no mistaking his intent. It is time to make the streets spill red.

Tommy takes hold of Sonia and sets the two goons who had been holding her to rush Dillon. Dillon rushes towards the pair in a full sprint, leaving them to adopt a slightly more confused look. The both of them recoil for a moment before pressing forward. Just a foot or so away from them Dillon drops to his knees and outstretches his arms and slams them forward into their legs, tripping both in the process. The one on his right tumbles into a parked car. The one on the left slams hard enough on the ground to have the wind knocked out of him. Dillon pops up and goes over to roll the winded one over with his foot before placing a boot on the man's throat, letting the full force of his weight quickly crush the man's throat with little effort on his part. The scrawny man claws at the boot cutting off his air supply, it is without reward, however. He can't seem to get a decent grip on the boot. The man who slammed into the car stands up and turns towards Dillon simply to catch Dillon's airborne tomahawk in his neck before falling over with a muffled scream gurgled with the blood rushing across his neck and down chest. Dillon puts enough force on his leg to hear a crunch from the man's throat he has his boot resting on. The windpipe and larynx now damaged far beyond repair. The man goes limp after briefly clutching Dillon's boot, making only a wheezing sound that is indicative of the pain, he must be in. Both men lays dying for a few miserable moments, seemingly incapable of moving.

As Tommy sees how quickly Dillon has taken care of the first two, he tells the other two to release the girls and the trio advance.

"Run! Go to my truck, it's around the corner. There are two friends of mine in there, you'll be safe. You do not want to see what comes next. Now GO!" Dillon shouts at the women. Something tells him that these three won't be as easy as the first two. He simply wants them to be more entertaining. Tommy stays in front of Dillon while the other two spread out around either side of him.

"You should have just kept walking D-Man. I don't want to do this after everything you've helped me and my brother out with," Tommy says keeping his attention up front.

"So maybe don't?" Dillon suggests with a gesture he knows is useless. "Or not." He grins as the two guys keep getting closer.

"I wish I didn't have to, but you don't know how Alex is now. He is worse than he ever was as gangbanger before the world went to shit," Tommy callously states throwing his hands up to gesture to this hell they have all wandered into a little more than two weeks ago. "He keeps us safe and some level of order, even in all this chaos. We just do as he says and don't question his orders, that's just how it is now." Dillon can't help but to smile wickedly after hearing this.

"So, you're all his bitches now is that it? Doing what you're told and being good little lap dogs?" Dillon scoffs as the smile creeping across his face seems to make him look even more frightening than Tommy found him on a good day. He makes a few clicks and whistles like he is calling a dog. He even barks once before letting loose a quick laugh. Tommy's remaining goons think he is crazy, and they start to relax and laugh a bit despite having witnessed him take down two of their own. Tommy knows better. The happier Dillon seems to become the more afraid Tommy grows.

"So, why the hell does Alex have you harassing Thad's family?"

"Oh hombre, if only you hadn't stepped in. Alex probably would have let you join us if you didn't cause too much trouble and take out two of his men," He is still trying to sell his old mentor on the idea. The boy is almost pleading, but for who? Tommy holds an open hand outstretched towards the two guys lying on the ground who are either dead or dying. "It's too late now though. I doubt even you would receive that much leniency from Alex." He shakes his head for a moment as he looks down at the ground. "You want to know what we were doing here, eh? No harm in telling you now, I mean you're going to die soon anyways."

"But Tommy, Alex said…" comes from one of the guys still circling Dillon

"Matt, shut the hell up!" Tommy snaps. "Alex, Dillon, and I go back a bit, I at least owe him this before we end him." The guy, Matt apparently, looks like the puppy you slapped for something he didn't realize he had done wrong. "We got word that Thad was shuttling some people we were looking for so we came to…to help them get back to us, but by the time we arrived Thad was taking them somewhere else, so we were trying to…persuade Jill and Sonia into telling us where that might be. You can see how well that was going." He tenderly runs a hand over the bleeding bite mark on his cheek, wincing in pain.

"I wasn't going to say anything, I just thought you had gotten with some freaky chick again and she was more than you could handle. Honestly man it's a bit of an improvement. If you live long enough for it to heal, assuming it doesn't get infected, you will have a cool scar to talk about. Who knows, maybe you could start a new post-end-of-the-world trend. Maybe I should get one." Dillon chuckles, a laugh devoid of humor and sanity. Entirely fake and forced. This causes a shiver to run up Tommy's back. Dillon can tell that the boy is hesitating.

"Come on Tommy! Let's waste this bastard and find those chicks so we can finish what we came here to do." Says the other guy, the shortest one of the group.

"Yeah Tommy, Come on. Finish me off." Dillon scoffs with a wicked twinkle in his eyes, a sight which freezes Tommy again. Something in that gaze disturbs Tommy for some unknown reason. Tommy cannot place his thumb on what has happened to Dillon in the last two weeks. There is a wildness, a savagery to his eyes that was not there before the world fell apart. That spark, whatever it is, sends an icy wave through Tommy's entire body.

"Finish me off like your sister use to. We can see if it is a family gift or simply one of her many learned skills. Maybe you can do it better, who knows? So why don't you come on over here and finish me off like the good little bitch you clearly are. There is this one thing she does with her tongue though that works like magic…"

That last remark seems to do it. Tommy is now far too pissed off to be cautious or afraid of Dillon. In fact, he seems more resolved and unflinching than he has during the whole exchange. His naturally tanned face turned a deep red as his anger boils over too seething hatred.

"Grab this bitch! I'll show him not to talk about my sister or any of my family like that!" Tommy roars moving fast with rage towards Dillon. He allows Matt and the other guy to grab either of his arms. They wrench his arms back, to the point that a normal person's shoulders would have been ruined. They kick the back of his knees so that he is kneeling on the ground in front of a pissed off Tommy. He reaches down and holds Dillon's face up with his left hand and proceeds to come down across his face with a hard punch.

"Come on! Hit me!" Dillon howls spitting out blood as he runs his tongue around his crimson mouth with an unnatural smile, "Hit me like a man! No more of these little girly punches!" Dillon screams madly at Tommy. Dillon's eyes are wide with excitement and glee. Dillon has let his darker side out again, giving it more freedom than it has had in years, possibly more freedom than he had ever permitted it outside of actual war. All the doors have been unlocked and the beast is free, fully free for the first time since his last overseas assignment. Although things this time are much different than overseas. No chain of command to report to or answer to. No more Laws of Armed Conflict or Rules of Engagement for him to follow. The only law left is the law of the jungle. The strong rule and survive while the weak die or serve. No one has managed to prove dominance over him yet, leaving him as the King of Jungle for the time being.

He is a very Mad King indeed, yet still a king

Tommy throws punch after punch, each more brutal than the last. Some hit him in the face while some are body shots. One of the guys holds Dillon's head up by pulling his hair back hard enough to almost rip some of it out. Dillon just laughs harder and harder, audibly losing his sanity with each blow as the laughs became more primal and eviler.

"Are you fucking insane dog?" Tommy pants as sweat runs down his cheek, mixing with the bloody bite to make a pink stream flowing from his jawline. "Matt, take over for a bit." He orders as he swaps places with the malicious youth. Tommy's knuckles are cut up and sore at this point. Dillon's laugh grows and worsens as the other two take turns beating him to a pulp. It evolves into an inhuman howl before long. When all three are panting with sweat flowing from their brow Dillon looks up at them, with the same defiant spark in his eyes.

"You girls aren't getting tired on me, yet are you?" He teases with a maniacal grin stretching from ear-to-ear. "Come on now, I still want to play some." He pleads as he stands up, knocking Tommy and Matt backwards as he does so. Their fists are too battered and bruised from dishing out blows to maintain a solid grip on him.

The look of terror replaces whatever had previously been on the boys' faces a moment before. Dillon jumps on the unnamed boy, landing on top of him as he falls. Dillon grabs the guy by the base of the skull, where it connects to the neck, and quickly bashed his head in four or five times with an ungodly amount of strength. This results in a wet crunch and blood pouring out from the rear of the boy's skull. Dillon only stops when someone behind him tackles him from behind, causing both to tumble away a bit. As the two men wrestled for advantage Dillon realizes it was Matt who had tackled him. This guy is more solid than Dillon had initially guessed. As they struggle Tommy rushes to help the third guy. An effort which at this point is a futile gesture. Tommy is too shocked to move as he tries to put the dude's brain back inside his caved in skull.

Dillon has managed to grab the boot knife he had tucked away and is trying to force it into Matt. The stocky young man is able to hold Dillon's hands and the blade just an inch or two above his face. Both grunting with effort as they partake in this sacred ceremony. The timeless and pure struggle for life. Nothing was ever more natural or as everlasting. Dillon feels more alive than he has in years, he feels an almost high sensation as his adrenal glands work double time. Pouring out massive quantities of his favorite little drug. The one high that is older than any marketed drug. The purest feeling that he has ever felt.

Dillon pulls back the knife, to Matt's premature relief. An elbow comes fast and devastatingly hard across the boy's jaw before he can collect himself. The pain only last a moment as Dillon drives his knife through Matt's eye and deep into his brain. Dillon can feel the blade scraping against the skull as it sinks into its target with a wet thud. Dillon twist the blade causing Matt's body to go still. Dillon is frozen in place for a moment as he watches the light in Matt's one good eye go out. There is a sort of high that some people get after killing another living creature. Hunter's know that kind of rush they get after bagging that incredible animal that you get once in a few years. That one kill that he will tell his drinking buddies repeatedly until he has a better one four or five years from then. Well, that is the rush that Dillon gets anytime he kills someone else when he is fighting. Only the feeling is magnified a few hundred times over. It is the knowledge that in the few moments of that struggle for life in death you have proven to be superior to your adversary. The ultimate form of competition. High stakes. Life and Death. The high from fighting alone was enough for Dillon, but when it escalated to a fight to the death. It is like going from just a few hits on the bong with your friends smoking the cheapest shit you could find to smoking an entire blunt of the highest quality weed around by yourself. It is that kind of jump.

He remains frozen for a few moments breathing heavily with excitement and a devilish grin running across his face. He stands up slowly after removing his knife and cleaning it on the boy's shirt. With a sigh he tosses his head back a bit and runs his hands through his lengthy hair. His hair now highlighted with streaks of crimson, make him look more deadly than any of these punk kids. With a cracking of his neck Dillon turns to face Tommy, who is still holding the boy who got his head smashed in. Dillon clears his throat to snap Tommy out of whatever panic he is in. Pure terror spreads across Tommy's face as he turns to see what has become of Matt. A bloody hole where his left eye had been, blood snaking its way down what is left of his face before cascading down to the street on either side of his head. Tommy's eyes dart up to Dillon who is slowly walking towards him now, a sadistic grin betraying an otherwise stoic face. This with the bloody streaks in his hair and the newly cleaned knife in his right-hand cause Tommy to panic more. The boy stumbles backwards on his hands and feet, tripping over the body he had just been so desperately trying to bring back to life.

"Please don't kill me man!" the coward cries sitting back on his knees as he throws his hand up in frail defense.

"I am not going to kill you as long as you tell me where Alex is." Dillon says as he pulls out zip ties set up like handcuffs. The gun tucked in the back of Tommy's waistband falls out amidst his hasty retreat. A flicker of hope runs through Tommy's eyes. Seeing this Dillon closes the distance in an instant. With a single kick he send Tommy rolling away from the pistol. Dillon leaps on the boy before he has a chance to recover. It only takes one descent punch for Dillon to render him unconscious. Dillon pulls out some zip ties and restrains the younger man. He throws the limp man over one shoulder with ease.

Chapter 9

Tampa, Florida

Mid-Afternoon, January 18th, 2030

2 Weeks into Hell

After Dillon restrains Tommy, he carries the drooling idiot to the truck where he gets everyone to walk into Pete's from the back entrance facing 11th avenue to escape the mid afternoon heat of south Florida. Dillon takes them this way, so they do not have to get too close to the bodies out front. Dillon is not sure how the girls might react to seeing the carnage up close. He wants to move them in fast so he can take care of a few things quick. He needs to get rid of the bodies before they begin to smell.

The decomposition process is only sped up under the heat of the scorching Florida sun.

It is what the smell would attract that concerns Dillon. Liz is tending to Jill and Sonia's minor injuries before she deals with the still drooling Tommy who has this oddly serene look on his face. Apparently, Liz had been a nurse prior to the apocalypse. The irony of the scene is not lost on Dillon. Aside from Jill and

Sonia witnessing him expediently dispatching the first two goons no one else but Dillon had been there to see what happened with the other three men. Given how Dillon looks and seems to have changed after this fight, no one can bring themselves to inquire as to what happened. The drooling, tied up, ass hat and his overall condition only further discouraged anyone from digging into what the details of the fight were.

The three-remaining people in the room who had known Dillon before the world went to shit knew that even on a good day you didn't want to mess with Dillon, even though he is an amazing person. Now with the rules of the world seemingly thrown out the window there is no telling what he is capable of. Jill is glad that she knew what Dillon's very limit moral code consisted of. It means that he would protect this little group of stragglers' no matter how much trouble it causes him. These are the same morals that told her Dillon is about to do something incredibly dumb in regard to Alex. Something both dangerous and frightening.

"While you're taking care of them, Frank and I are going to clean up outside." Dillon mutters into her ear. His hand rests briefly on Liz's shoulder causing her to get all red in the face. Dillon doesn't seem to notice as he keeps walking, grabbing Frank by the shirt collar out the door. Jill notices Liz getting flustered and the corner of Jill's mouth slightly curve upward. There seems to be something beneath the otherwise silent rage emanating from Dillon. Something darker.

Everyone else can sense it and seems to be frightened a bit because of that unease flowing out from him. A terrifying calm if you will.

Frank can't help but to throw up all over the street once the guys come within in few feet of where the fight had been. The smell of hot rotting meat has already started to seep from the bodies as they fried on the smoldering pavement. Dillon walks by as if not noticing the doorman losing his lunch. It seems as though Dillon is unable to smell anything. Once he has emptied his stomach and wiped his mouth Frank makes his way over to the car, giving the bodies considerable distance to avoid seeing or smelling the bodies. Dillon still doesn't seem to notice Frank's discomfort. He had lost any aversion to this kind of tuff a long time ago. Right this moment he is only thinking of what a waste it had been for these boys to have so hastily thrown their lives away. *Granted,* Dillon thinks to himself, *I probably didn't have to kill all four of them.* He shrugs off that notion as he sets to work with the task at hand. He starts by removing his tomahawk and cleaning it. On the victim's clothes.

Frank isn't sure what to make of what he sees when he emerges from Pete's garage where he had just parked the truck. The sun is now close to setting, casting an amber filter across the world. Everything looks like he is in some post-apocalyptic movie, which he basically is in. He comes upon the silhouette of Dillon rummaging through the bodies.

"What the hell are you doing?" Frank fearfully inquires as he walks up to Dillon, choking back every urge to barf all over again.

"I am stripping them of anything that we might need, this just includes their clothes. See." He says with a quick nod to the small pile of items a few feet away. "Now help me take of his pants." Dillon orders like that is a normal thing to do. Frank reluctantly does as he is asked, trying to just hold in whatever food is left inside of him.

After Dillon and Frank have finished pillaging the bodies Dillon piles up the bodies. Frank is growing more confused and disgusted with what he is seeing until Dillon lights the corpses on fire. Frank is somewhat disturbed by how none of this seemed to even phase Dillon.

"Why are we um, burning these bodies?" Frank asks, even more confused than a moment ago. Why would Dillon take care of the bodies like this when he was the one who killed them?

"I'm sure they weren't bad guys, just following the orders of a bad guy. Also, it helps to prevent the spreading of any diseases that could take refuge on rotting corpses. Plus, this way they won't draw in…" Dillon stops himself on the verge of letting the cat out of the bag. He recovers by saying. "anything that might want to feast on it. You can go inside and check on the others, I will stay out here and make sure these burn safely. Oh, but please take all that stuff with you." He points to the pile of pilfered items.

Frank is really taken aback by what Dillon is saying, for a moment the man sounds almost sympathetic, yet also unaffected by what had happened. His lips edge up in a faint smile as he walks inside as he sees a glimmer of the man he had come to know before the world's end.

Dillon stares into the flames that have now engulfed the bodies and the pallets he had dragged from a nearby alley for fuel. Sitting down on the street curb he listens to the now predominately silent city. The silence both excites and perplexes him. Is Tampa the only area to be hit like this, he wonders. He can't tell but, the fact that there has been no aid up until this point makes him feel like this is much bigger than just the city. Nationwide? Maybe even worldwide. It is impossible to say at this point.

There's a small, ever growing part of him who is perfectly fine with things being how they are and this being a worldwide phenomenon. The same part that was clawing for more and more mental real estate. The voice inside that preaches this is a more simplified way of things, which it is. It returns people to survival of the fittest. A most primal and natural law which humanity seemed to have superseded long ago. *We became more like demons than gods*, Dillon thinks to himself. He thinks of how insatiably humans had killed and devoured the once plentiful bounty of the natural world. Humans have perfected the art of killing. The young ecologist still deep inside proclaims this is better than the impending mass extinction that humanity would have caused.

Dillon is so busy contemplating the predicament they are all in that before he realizes it the bodies have pretty much burned down to bones and the pallets are now a pile of ash. The sun had set about ten minutes ago he thinks as he looks up and sees how dark the sky has grown. There is now just a faint glow on the horizon as the planet turns them into night and the moon begins to shine.

He turns to walk inside when a flurry of movement from the side of his vision catching his attention. Dillon spins around so quickly and silently that not even his boots make a sound. Scanning the street for any signs of life. He feels the hairs on the back of his neck stand on end and a surge of electricity course through his body as every muscle prepares for a fight he feels coming. For the first time in almost two weeks he feels the old familiar hooks of Fear sink into him. The street is silent, and beyond some pieces of trash blowing in the breeze it is devoid of motion. Was it one of the creatures? Maybe someone from Alex's group? Not knowing what it is causes more anxiety than anything else. Uncertain if he could ward off one of those… monsters he had witnessed from the protection of his lofty apartment. Even less sure if the old brick building could keep them out for long. He is really hoping it was his minds playing tricks on him, paranoia that emerges from constantly being on edge all day for many days in a row. Something which he had both witnessed and experienced over many deployments. He doesn't have much time to contemplate these questions. A door behind him opens, casting an outline of light into the darkened street.

"Dillon, you ever coming in? you've been out here for a long time by yourself." Liz says with a forced playfulness to her voice as she tries to hold on to some semblance of normalcy amidst all the chaos of the day, the worry she feels is echoed beneath the cheery facade.

"What's wrong?" she asks as she walks up and places a hand on his arm, effectively snapping him out of it. His hand suddenly darts up to catch her wrist. Both soon drop after he realizes what he has just done.

"Are you alright?" worry beginning to creep back into her voice. His eyes once again scanning their surroundings.

"I…I'm f-fine. Just thought…thought I saw something a moment ago." He stammers out, still feeling foggy and in a haze. Liz can't help but feel like he is still lost in thought even as he responds to her. "Must have just been my mind playing tricks on me, it's been a long day. Hasn't it?" He says with a most insincere smile. The flat, forced kind of someone trying to reassure another even when they themselves are anything but okay.

"It has been a long day indeed Dillon. Why don't you come in now and I can look at your scratches," She licks her thumb and slides it over a small scratch on his forehead to remove a drop of blood. She totally just mommed him. Her face turns a cherry shade of red as she realizes this. He is a little to fried to notice. Wiping her hand on her pants before carrying on. "Then we can all rest for the night."

"Alright Liz." He sounds exhausted to her as an odd softness takes root in his voice that was not there a moment ago.

A softness which for some reason seems to fluster Liz and makes her turn abruptly before walking back inside to hide how badly she is blushing. She can feel the heat rising in her cheeks and is certain they are almost scarlet in color by now. The stir it causes in her leads her to thoughts much too romantic and soft for this new, harsher world. Or at least that what she convinces herself of.

"Why are you so red?" Frank ask when Liz comes back in through the door. Liz snaps her head up from staring at the floor, caught off guard.

"What? Oh, no reason just feeling a little flushed after today." She nervously lies, Frank pretends to believe her even though the thin grin that takes root says he knows better than that. She punches him like women do sometimes when they are flustered or don't like what you said regardless of the truth behind the words. Frank winces, mostly for show to make her feel good about. He also doesn't want her to hit him for real, he is not very tough when it comes to taking hits. Frank understands where she was coming from though. He thinks Dillon is amazing. That man is probably the only reason any of them were alive right now. But even before all this ugliness there was always something about the way Dillon carried himself that seemed to make people feel three kinds of ways about him. They either respected him, feared him, or saw him as an adversary because of the obvious strength he seemed to have, both mentally and physically.

Dillon comes in a minute or two after Liz had come in. Dillon seems to have his mind elsewhere in an anxious way.

"We need to make sure we barricade all the entrance points on the ground." He absent-mindedly mumbles as he shuffles towards a seat at the bar. It doesn't seem like the Dillon they all knew. Sure, he would seem far off sometimes, but there would be a sadness about him in those moments. There is no sadness in his vacancy right now, only tension and worry. A sort of nervous electricity. This in turn makes the rest of the group slightly nervous, yet the cause of the tension is unknown to everyone else. They are all wary of whatever it was that could cause this otherworldly man to seem so, preoccupied. Dillon just sits there, mind clearly adrift in thought while Liz tends to his injuries. Most of them are minor. All except for what looks like claw marks on his calves from where one of the men was scratching in a desperate attempt to remove the boot from his own throat. This one looks deep enough that Liz needed to do stitches.

"Hey Dillon, I am going to have to stitch up the scratches on your leg. This is probably going to hurt since I don't have anything to numb it up, okay?" he doesn't seem to notice, but consents with a simple nod of his head. She rolls up his pant leg after removing the weapons in the way. She pours some liquor on it to clean it and Dillon does not even wince like a normal person would have. She keeps a wary eye on him as she heats up the needle with a lighter to sterilize it. He has the same non-expressive reaction when she begins stitching his leg up. She pauses about two or three inches in to take a few swigs of vodka to calm her nerves and steady her hands so that she can do a better job stitching him up. All total there are about 25 or so stitches in his leg now. The fact that it is not her best job is evident by the blood dripping down his leg.

This hardened looking man still doesn't seem to notice anything has happened. Dillon is somewhere else, another time all together. What seems like a life time ago. Back when he went to a hell even worse than this. It has been a little over a decade since then. Even after all the attempts to forget, all the booze, all the drugs, all the sex. Even after everything those images are still seared into his mind.

Chapter 10

March 13th, 2018   Almost 12 years ago

0930 Eastern Standard Time

Presidential War Room, Beneath the White House

All the people are already present and seated by the time he arrives. They are all arguing amongst themselves. There is a silver crowned man with a gut that just slightly pokes the front of his suit out, Secretary of Defense, who is about ready to start a fist fight with the Secretary of State. He is using a lot of colorful language in a rather creative way. The sentence structure is so unique it is causing the Secretary of State to pause out of confusion, not even close to comprehending the obscenities being flung her way. In the shadows of the centrally lit room there is a buzz. A swarm of various aids, assistants and countless other crucial people who will never be recognized zoom around taking care of many tasks that need tended to while the big dogs bark around the poker table.

The man standing in the shadowy doorway is suddenly glad he popped as many painkillers as he did. He already knows he will have a mountain of a headache when he leaves this room in a few hours. *Yeah right.* He tells himself. *I will be lucky to be home in time for dinner, the wife is not going to be happy about this. Again.* Shaking off the insurmountable sense of foreboding the man in the doorway walks into the dimly lit room, heading directly towards his chair. The last empty seat at the end of the table. He is about half way there before someone sees him and calls the room to attention.

"Relax it's just me. Keep working." Never one for ceasing the flow productivity. The buzz picks right back up again. That's one of the things he isn't exactly crazy for in this job. Everyone stops what they are doing the second they see him, and they all have to treat him differently. In his eyes he is just a man. Just as capable of faulty judgement and falling as everyone else in this messed up world. He has no idea what he is doing the majority of the time yet they expect him to have answers causing him to stretch the narrative to save himself. "What's the story General Yeager?" he says to one of the boots in the room.

The slender silver haired fox of a man in an Army issued uniform stiffens before standing to confront the man from the doorway.

"Well, Mr. President, it seems all the forces we had trained and supported in Syria have been removed from play sir." The president's face seems to drain of any and all color for a second before he manages to regain his composure. Carrying on while the President regains some color back to his normally orange face, "All of them taken out in a series of coordinated attacks with in the last two hours." The tan, leather faced General pauses before continuing at the silent behest of the President. "Sir, there was a problem beyond that." *Yay! Just what I need, more issues.* The man thinks ever so sarcastically. This obnoxious sarcasm is the only way he can attempt to keep a cool head in this shit storm of a morning briefing. "There were European forces at some of these encampments that were hits, sir." The general grows ever more nervous by every word. "The French, the British, the Belgian, and the Italian's just to name a few. Sir nearly the whole of Europe is ready to go to war right now." The President can't help but let his face betray how fucked he believes this situation to be.

"And who is taking credit for the attacks, ISIS? Or is it Assad and his people?" the General shares a sullen look with the rest of the table, "God Dammit man! Tell me who has claimed the credit for this massacre?!" The President slams the table with both hands clenched tightly as his patience is running exceedingly low. A strand of his oddly golden colored hair falls in front his face. He quickly tucks his hair back into place trying to minimalize how disheveled he looks right this moment. He is certain that it doesn't help very much. He most definitely looks like a hot mess.

"Sir, Its all of them sir. ISIS, the Russians, the Iranians, some Iraqi Militia, and every known terrorist group that has an axe to grind against the United States and our allies. They are each claiming different attacks. ISIS is claiming credit for most of them. Russia and Iran pulled their support for the UN an hour ago. Sir, people are shouting, pleading for war. And that's members of the UN Securities Council. The same people who were previously working towards peace are now the ones ringing the bells of war." The General has started to jab a finger into the desk with each new sentence he finishes. That poor finger looks like it is going to break at any moment. Not knowing what else do he brings both hands to his face in anguish and stress. Barely in office a few months and War World Three seems to be knocking at his door. *Fuck.* That the only word floating around his head. "Sir? What are we going to do sir?" the Lost sounding man asks his President. The entire room is deathly silent as all eyes turn to him. The weight of the uncertain and impending conflict pushing down on everyone. It is several moments more before the President looks up. His look of despair is now washed away by an expression of confidence.

"Put out word to the rest of the UN not to make any actions out of such impulsive anger. But make sure it sounds better than that. Tell them I want to establish a coalition force. No drafts, no orders. This is a strictly voluntary assignment for any military member who wants to go fight. We have to fight a small-scale war to avoid any more civilian deaths. Make sure these men and women who volunteer understand this will be war that they are volunteering to wade into. Not war like we have fought the last few decades. This one is likely going to be more up close and personal than that. Make sure they know there are very real chances that they will not make it back." The worker bees in the background have resumed buzzing around with renewed frenzy as they begin to carry things out as fast he speaks.

"I only want experienced men and women from our forces. All specialties are applicable. No less than three years, if they are close to the end of a contract this will require them to reenlist if they want to go. Begin vetting and training immediately. I want them ready last week." The Generals all nod in a mix of grim and eager expressions. "Send word to every nation that I don't want this leaving these boundaries," He says as he circles an area on a map near him. "Tell them that anything outside of this will be a direct act of war against the United States itself. I will not tolerate any act of war towards this nation. This limit goes for every side involved." Slamming his right hand down on the table he slides the map to the Secretary of Defense with his other hand. "And I want this quiet. Absolutely zero media coverage. I don't even want to hear mention of it on some college blog. This is all silent until we are done." Everyone pauses again. Staring at him in anticipation for more. Standing up and slamming down both hands "What the fuck are you people waiting for? Move your asses!"

Chapter 11

Tampa, Florida

January 18, 2030   Just after 5pm

2 weeks into hell.

Inside Stinky Pete's Bar

Liz isn't sure what to do. None of them are. Frank still looks like he is sick and Dillon, well… Dillon has the expression of someone who is reliving some very traumatic very real memories. It seems to Liz like something that had happened outside had somehow triggered something within Dillon. Flipping on the switch labeled *"Trauma"*. Dillon finds himself sitting alone in a dark room. The only things in it are himself strapped to a chair and an old school projector blowing up bright images of every terrible thing he has ever witnessed or gone through. This is how it always starts when he suffers through one of these anxiety episodes. He is forced to relive all the negativity in his life. Part of this is his fault. He shoves any sense of feeling deep down, every move and action choreographed. Periodically it will all overflow, either in fits of rage or crippling attacks like this one.

Liz can't help feeling relieved. She knows that it is wrong and just a little sick to be almost comforted by the fact that Dillon is suffering. Their savior. The stranger who had saved her ass on the street just several days before. The enigma she has been living with this last week. That Dillon was showing just how human he can be. Even underneath all that…all that perfection which seems to make up Dillon he is still just a man who can be as haunted by his own demons as anyone else might. She is however terrified to even try imagining what could make this war god of man seem so vulnerable.

"Hey Dillon. Hey, are you alright man?" comes Frank from across the room as he has started to regain some color in his face. He is walking across the room. Right over to Dillon. "What happened after I came inside man?" he wonders aloud as he places a hand on the man's shoulder. This seems to startle Dillon as he jumps from the human contact and seems to dodge away from Frank as though he had tried to punch him rather than attempt to comfort his friend. His eyes still show that he isn't there as he grabs Frank by the collar and lifts him in the air with ease. His lips parted to show his perfect teeth clenched together as he breathes heavily through his mouth. His eyes are wilder and more animalistic than those of a man.

"Whoa dude." Frank exclaims as he throws his hands up. A gesture of peace. An effort to show he means no harm. Fear and pain spread across the doorman's face smoother than butter on hot toast. "It's alright. I'm just trying to make sure you are alright." The young man says in a soothing voice. He knows he has broken through to Dillon when he is returned to the ground.

Regret is the first thing Dillon feels as he comes back from *Then*. He sees the looks of fear and concern on everyone's face. Well, Tommy just looks like he is about to shit his pants, he looks so scared. Frank thinks it even smells like the guy has crapped himself.

　　　Remorse falls over Dillon almost immediately. "Sorry guys. I wasn't trying to scare anyone, I was just…. Just, never mind. I'm sorry Frank." As these last few muddled words leave his mouth his face contorts again with pain of old memories. This temporary revelation of Dillon's own humanity and personal demons only frightens them further. A few of them had been eager to see him once a again display normal emotions, regardless of what emotion. They now wished he were still as stoic as he had been a few minutes ago. Shaking off the nightmares of his past like a shiver has run down his spine Dillon recomposes himself.

　　　"Alright Tommy, care to tell us where Alex and the rest of his gang of idiots are?" a recomposed Dillon asks as he turns to the restrained man sitting several feet away on the floor. All eyes turn to Tommy. Tommy simple shakes his head, his terror riddled eyes never leaving the chunk of floor between his feet. "I need an answer Tommy." Dillon presses with raised voice.

　　　"I can't man. You have no idea what he does to traitors." Tommy quivers as he brings his glance up to Dillon's boots.

　　　Dillon lets out an impatient sigh. They find Dillon's face is entirely devoid of emotion as they turn to face him. Eyes going back and forth like spectators at a tennis match. "Fine Tommy. That's okay. I understand, I really do." A false sense of empathy is over played as he speaks. "You've seen what he does to people. You are scared to endure the same pain." Tommy vacantly nods as he recalls the scenes of punishment. A traumatized look is painted on his face. The young man is clearly torn about the violent acts he has so willing witnessed. Dillon leans down so his chin is within Tommy's line of sight.

Kirtland D. Neal

"I want you to remember this moment Tommy. I want you to remember the last time I asked you nicely." Dillon growls just loud enough for the others to hear him. His lips instinctively curl up to expose teeth like a dangerous dog's. An ice-cold shiver shoots up everybody else's backs as their skin crawls in fear. Tommy starts to twist and jerk as he tries to flee Dillon. The large man reaches back and brings a heavy right cross down upon the captive's head. Tommy slumps over as he is rendered unconscious.

Everyone else in the room looks at each other, not a single one is able to think of something useful to do or say. Every mouth hangs slightly open in shock. Dillon picks up Tommy and throws him over his shoulder like a bag of dog food. Effortlessly and silent. Dillon carries the rag doll out to the garage where the truck, and more importantly his tools are stored. As he passes the most average and sturdy looking table at the bar he reaches over and drags the chair behind him. The screeching noise of the wooden legs dragging against the cold concrete floor is the only thing to cut through the silence. The scuff marks from the legs are almost unnoticeable on the old slab. No one else is moving or talking. They are frozen in uncertainty.

Having tied Tommy to the chair Dillon pops back in the main area, a beat-up old box is held precariously in his left hand. "You guys are going to want to put these on. I will you know when you're alright to remove 'em." He says as he drops the box of earplugs and headsets on the floor in between them all before turning back out towards the garage. The silence is soon filled with the thunderous roar of a speaker playing old school rock and roll. It's time to see if Dillon still has the *skills* that he had utilized those many years after he came back from hell the first time. To see if the old Dillon is still dead in that old hell. Check if the beast left in his absence had grown complacent from a few years of inactivity. Dillon first removes Tommy's clothes before duct taping his wrist and ankles to the chair. A cargo strap secures his chest to the chair. Dillon lightly slaps Tommy several times trying to wake him up.

"Alright Tommy," Dillon starts as Tommy reals back to the land of the living after sputtering off the bucket of water Dillon had tossed on him.

"You have one final chance to avoid any more pain. Where is Alex and why does he want Thad?"

"I can't." he pleads more with his pathetic eyes than his words. "Alex kills you slowly after making you watch everything you care about get destroyed. He breaks you before killing you." The end is hard to make out past the rising sobs as rivers of tears began to cascade down his cheeks, forming a series of mini waterfalls.

"Okay Tommy, ok. Just remember you chose this." Dillon utters in disappointment. Turning to one of the duffel bags set around them, a circle Tommy had not noticed until now. Dillon kneels for a moment or two in order to rummage around the bag before rising with his prize. A double leather latched gag. The red ball that was the mouthpiece was now only a dull sheen of its former candy apple shine, covered in bite marks from countless uses. Both malicious and sensual. There are two faded leather straps on each side, the two on the left have small buckles like a belt. They are somewhere between black and brown with the stress cracks that leather sometimes got. There is also an additional band over the ball so that it has leather straps on three sides to hold it in place.

Tommy begins to twist and jerk to try and escape him as Dillon tries to place the gag on him. This effort proves useless as Dillon back hands him before continuing to put the gag on him. Tommy's ears fit between the straps on either side almost perfectly. This makes them rather hard to get out of when one is restrained as Tommy is.

Tommy no longer recognizes the man who is rising from one of the duffel bags with a syringe filled with an opaque liquid, a hand full of sticks, a mallet, and pliers. The man still has the physical appearance of Dillon Thompson, but it is no longer the same man. The eyes. Dillon's eyes, while guarded and slightly anxious, have always had a lively warm shine to them. This is not the case with the man now approaching Tommy. There is nothing in his eyes. They are icy and desolate. Lifeless and cruel. If someone were superstitious like Tommy's grandma and had the misfortune of seeing these eyes, they would probably call them *Ojos del Diablo,* the Eyes of the Devil. The same sadistic maliciousness associated with the fallen angel fills the depths of Dillon's eyes. Tommy does not have the luxury of believing in the fairy tales of religion. But he can now see clear as day that true evil can and does exist in this world. Evil far beyond what Alex seems capable of. An evil that is born of light being broken and corrupted. A black hole staring back from where a star had once burned bright. The true demons of the world are no mystical or mythical creatures, as Tommy will soon find out, the real demons are human beings themselves. The only known entity with such an insatiable appetite for death and destruction. In hindsight it made perfect sense to Tommy if he looked back at countless tyrants in history or even just observed how man has treated the planet and her inhabitants.

"This magical concoction is a personal recipe." Dillon proudly announces over the blare of the radio. "It slightly lowers your heart rate, so you won't have a heart attack from the stress and make every touch a thousand times more sensitive." Tommy can see an evil shine to his eyes as he looks down on the man. "A pin prick will feel like you've been stabbed by a steak knife. It also makes your blood clot a faster, so you hopefully wont bleed out as fast as normal. I call this bad boy Misery Loves Company, or MLC for short. He will be your worse enemy, well after me of course." A malevolent smile flickers across his face for the briefest of moments as he finishes the final sentence.

After placing the other items on the ground in front of Tommy he walks around the back of the chair just out of his line of sight. Pulling Tommy's head back in a less than comfortable manner, to reveal his neck. Dillon clinically uses the needle to punctures his jugular, the plunger steadily depressed until not a drop is left in the syringe. Dillon tapes a small piece of gauze over the few droplets of blood that come out of the wound. Dillon holds two fingers over the other side of Tommy's neck, waiting the two minutes it takes for drug to take effect and lower his heart rate. Eyes on his watch the whole time. The world seems to hold still for Tommy as the terror begins to set in and the few minutes seem like hours.

Seeming pleased after it only takes about 90 seconds, Dillon doubles back around to pick up what Tommy thought were simply sticks. They are in fact sharpened bamboo shoots. About a foot long each. Most are about a quarter of an inch in diameter. There are 21 sticks in all. Dillon grabs the notably darker stick which also seems to be a bit thicker than the rest. He puts the other sticks on a metal tray on a stand next to them. Like those trays they have at the dentist office.

[God, Dentist. There is a reason why children are naturally afraid of those guys. Seriously, who thinks "I want to spend the rest of my life sticking my fingers and tools in stranger's mouths to clean up after the filthy bastards." Clearly not the sanest individuals out there. If you are a dentist…. I'm sorry.]

Dillon places a flat board under Tommy's right hand and tapes it down so the edge of each finer is just at the end of the wood. Picking up the hammer Dillon takes special care to pound away at each finger on Tommy's hand. Tommy experiences this heightened pain in slow motion, tears begin to flow down even stronger and his screams are muffled by the gag in his mouth. After ensuring that all the bones are broken in his right hand, Dillon positions the hammer behind the flat end of the dark stick he has selected, the opposite end gently touching Tommy's fingertip where nail meets the flesh. Dillon begins to gently hammer upward into the nail on the man's thumb, causing the nail to rise and separate from the digit. There is of course some extra flesh that is dragged away with the nail itself. He continues nailing until the nail is only holding on by the back of the cuticle. It rocks back and forth like an open flap of a cardboard box. Swapping the hammer and steak for the pliers he rips the nail off. Tommy's persistent and muffled howls go unnoticed by Dillon. The pained response is nothing more than white noise to Dillon. Dillon picks up two large containers the Tommy hadn't see before. They are labeled *Pepper Powder & Salt* and *Lemon juice/hot sauce.* He pours them into some plastic disposable shot cups, like they ones they make Jell-O shots in. Each item in its own cup. He also mixes enough to soak the other wooden steaks in a Tupperware container. Dillon lets the finger soak in a small cup of the juice before drying the wound off with the salt. Tommy endures this agony for each and every finger and toenail. If not for his chemically lowered heart rate he would have most definitely had a heart attack, just on the first hand. Dillon wipes off the hands and feet to make sure they are easy to grip.

   Dillon swaps the dark steak for its lighter siblings and nails each one of the soaked sticks in the tips of every newly declawed digit. They are positioned below where the nail had previously rested, the center of the fingertip. He drives the sticks in far enough so that he can see the bulge beneath the skin in the hands and feet. All of Tommy's toes and fingers are effectively and rather painfully immobilized. Dillon looks up as he notices Tommy seems to relax. Dillon for a moment grows concerned that the boy has grown numb to the pain already. Looking at Tommy's face Dillon can see that is not the case thankfully. The rest of their conversation would not be as productive if that happened. Sadly, though he did pass out from the pain when Dillon thought he was relaxing. The young man looks agonized even in sleep as sweat flows down every inch of skin on his face, he wears a mask of severe pain. Dillon looks at his watch to find that ninety minutes has already come and gone since they both started this little adventure. Wiping off the slight sweat on his own brow with his forearm, Dillon pauses while he contemplates how to proceed from here.

Not one to leave a job unfinished, Dillon finishes with everything before stopping and wrapping up the fingertips to prevent any bleeding out or worse, getting infected. The infection might kill Tommy before Dillon got the answers he is searching for. Dillon lets him rest as he cleans up the slight mess around them before pressing on. Grabbing a black canvas bag from the duffel, Dillon throws it over Tommy's head after hooking up a mp3 blasting heavy metal. Dillon had learned and relearned many times that sensory deprivation is essential to these kinds of "interviews".

After cleaning up and securing Tommy's restraints Dillon turns the radio off and walks back inside. Everyone is still sitting around anxiously and staring at the ground, only now they are all wearing the headsets he had provided. Liz notices him first. She shoots up fast enough that she sees the fuzzy black and white dots that tell her she needs to slow down. Her anxiety and impatience had long since run out.

"So?" she inquires, fearfully optimistic. "What did he say?" the rest of the group is removing their headsets and approaching Dillon as she is.

"He hasn't said anything since I gagged him about an hour and a half ago." He coldly returns as he grabbed a bar rag and proceeded the wipe away the blood which covers more of him than he had originally realized. Everyone is terrified, looking at him the same way a child appears when the see Pennywise for the first time. "I gave him a final chance to avoid any more… discomfort. He obviously turned down that proposal." Dillon can't contain his joy as a smirk flashes across his face before disappearing. "He is resting now, but I don't want any of you to go in there. He needs some alone time to reflect on his choices." He calmly explains, trying to regain the lightness he normally adopts around people. "Before you ask its more for you than him. You guys won't know what to do if you see what is back there. I didn't back when I first…." He trails off as that far off look returns. Only momentarily this time though as he quickly shakes off the look before carrying on. Like a glitch in programming.

"Any of you guys know how to shoot a gun?"

Chapter 12

Syria, fifty miles outside of Aleppo

August 21st, 2018

A few months into war

Amidst a war torn country arrives the newly formed American Joint Branches Assault Taskforce, which is being called the J-BAT's by the big wigs in D.C., a name which is quickly adopted by the rest of the general population.

The J-BAT's are fighting their first battle since they had arrived in country a little over a week before. This battle progresses grudgingly slow. Dragging along as fast as the tectonic plates reshape the planet's surface. Due to the unknown number of civilians still scattered across the region there is to be no air support short of intel gathering. This means it is back to old school war tactics. This means there will almost definitely be a drastic increase in casualties for the US forces.

Kirtland D. Neal

Sergeant Jacobson had been a Sergeant in the Army prior to joining the BATs, so he is a little unsure of how to feel about being placed under some Air Force guy. Technical Sergeant Thompson had been a Staff Sergeant in the Air Force before this. He was an aircraft mechanic, not even a proper soldier in Jacobson's eyes. Yet this wrench turner had somehow been selected to lead the small detachment. Thompson had also been rumored to be the next first shirt whenever the current one left. This only further infuriated Jacobson.

Jacobson had been 18 when he joined the Army just several years prior. This coupled with his upbringing as an Army brat basically meant he had grown up in the military in every sense. He had gotten to the point where he was convinced, he was the pinnacle of what it meant to be a soldier. In the clean-shaven buzz cut box that he had grown accustomed to viewing everything and everyone this man in front of him did not match anything else. This contrast bothered the Sergeant so deeply it left him bitter and scornful. A man who had his pride stepped on when he was placed under the direction of another who was, as far as he could see, unfit to lead a dog on a walk let alone an entire unit. Thompson, in Jacobson's opinion, was far too laxed and lenient with the men in the unit as well as the day to day handlings of everything. His age begot him nothing in regard to sternness.

Thompson has heard murmurs back at base that a handful of the men are less than approving of his appointment to this position. There are 100 men in the JBAT's 3rd division. Thompson has neither the time nor the patience to seek out the malcontents. He has ordered the men under him to look after one another like brothers, something that should have been instilled since basic military training and hammered in with a sledgehammer over the course of their careers so far. Yet even despite this there is still countless cases in the traditional branches of service men and women not looking after each other like family.

Apocalypse Virus: Initial Infection

"At the end of the day all you have is family," his father's old words came forth from his lips as he addressed the 3rd after everyone had first arrived at the base. "Here you are all family. That means whether you like, love, hate, or resent each other you look after one another. That's what defines a family. Not how much they get along, but rather by how they come together to take care of and protect the family." Some of the troops still seemed lost so he pressed further, "Your main priority should be to accomplish all missions we are sent on. However, I present you with my own tasking. At the end of the day, regardless of mission success or failure, your main purpose here should be to make sure that each and every one of the ugly mugs sitting around you make it back here at the end of those missions so they can get back to their families. You fight for each other. You do this and I will fight tooth and nail against anyone who might try and come down on you. This is my end of this deal, to give everything I must protect my family. Even if I need to protect it from other parts of the family." He had no speech written down, this awesome movie scene type speech came straight out his ass. That is one of his best qualities. He excels under pressure no matter how ill prepared. This self-belief may soon prove fatal. "Alright! We roll out for our first mission tomorrow morning at 0600. Hurry up and get settled in and try and catch some sleep tonight. Dismissed." He walks away to get a better briefing for the mission the next day.

Chapter 13

January 19th,2030

0130 hours

Tampa, Florida

Dillon Thompson

After a lengthy lesson on how to use and maintain a firearm Frank and the girls wonder off to bed, leaving Dillon downstairs sitting alone at the bar. A scene which has progressively claimed more and more of his time over the many long years. He stares at the half empty glass of whiskey in his hand, pausing between sips as he mulls over everything that has happened since the whole damn world swan dived down the toilet bowl. Not even bothering to circle the bowl before plunging into the warmth of the abysmal sewers. Those abominations he had seem from up in his apartment flash through his mind. Suddenly he realizes what he has forgotten.

Dillon sets to work on turning the bar into as much of a fortress as he can, trying his best not to wake the others too much. Granted with how many bar fights he has been in while Sonia slept upstairs completely unaware he is confident that he won't have to be too quiet. He manages to board up the windows quickly

enough after cannibalizing a few of the spare tables in the garage.
Dillon makes sure to smack the prisoner awake with each visit.
After some scavenging and adjusting he comes up with enough
metal braces to install them on the front and back doors that each
hold a massive, heavy beam in place like those old castle doors.
With sweat now covering his body he decides to take a break as
he pours himself another double shot of whiskey on the rocks. He
is suddenly grateful for that hurricane about a decade back that
prompted Thad to ask for Dillon's help with installing solar panels
on the roof and some back-up generators around back. Dillon
grabs the hand towel he had left on the bar earlier to now wipe the
sweat off his brow as he settles into his seat at the bar. He sees
just how quickly the time has gone by since he had started
fortifying Pete's as he gazes down at his watch to find that is
already 0300. It is far from a fortress, but it will make do as one
hell of a hurricane shelter. He is confident that anything shy of a
Cat-5 could tear this bitch down. The question was how strong are
those things?

It is almost a solid two hours and far too many drinks later
he staggers his way back towards his room. The drunk bastard
trips over some of his tools on the way there, slamming into the
wall sending a slight tremor throughout the building. This causes
Jill and the others to stir a bit. They wake just enough to register
what woke them and venture out of their rooms cautiously
searching for what shook the building. They follow the trail of
open doors and lights which lead them just outside of Dillon's
room. A slim streak of sweat on the opposite wall highlights his
progress down the corridor. 10 minutes have easily passed since
he collided with the building. Plenty of time for his silent spiral to
have reached its full swing.

Dillon is sitting at the edge of his bed in his favorite of the
drunken rooms, a sideways glass gives way to the stream of
spilled whiskey. An amber reflection of the tortured man mimics

everything the original does. Hands are pressed into his eyes trying to force the pain back inside of his skull. The bones quiver as though everything he has ever felt is attempting to rush out in every direction, all at once. The alcohol has failed to numb him tonight. Those same hands slide up to grab on those thick brown bangs of his. The only show of years of nightmares are a handful of silver streaks highlighting the mane of burnt sienna. As his hands leave his eyes, the ocean of tears he was holding back now flood forth. The salt riddled river cascades down cheekbones and his jawline until they freefall over the mattress and down to the floor below. His mouth opens so wide it feels as though his jaw will break away and fall off. Every muscle across his head, neck and chest strain to their limits. The taught cords and blood vessels bulge against his skin. He pulls so hard on those deep brown locks that it feels as though he is being ripped from every angle inside and out. Just as all of this hits a peak a silent scream shakes him to the core. A howl only audible to himself. The tortured moan is only interrupted by the snot induced huffing and puffing as it picks up its pace. Snot, sweat, and tears flow down his face.

He spirals from dry eyed to complete and debilitating sobbing. He doubles over, grabbing his knees in an effort to hold himself together. He is being attacked by everything. All the people who have either left or died along the way. It gets impossible to breath for him now. He is overwhelmed by his own existence. He remembers every flaw he has ever had. Every mistake or terrible choice he has ever made up until this point. All the anger, sadness, and weakness he has ever felt coming rushing back, brand new and fresh again. As fresh as the moment he felt all of this. He is reminded of all the times he was toxic. The poison which has plagued so many people over the years. Remembering every single time, he was almost strong enough to end this miserable excuse for an existence he calls a life.

Why? Why have I never been good enough to make a difference? Because you are just some small, weak, useless man who could never be anything but toxic. You are POWERLESS! There is a reason why no one is willing to stand by your side. You are a bomb that they are waiting to watch blow the fuck up! They've always known what kind of parasite you are. Nothing more than amusement for them. You are lucky they even let you stay around. Why do they always leave me? Why am I so incapable of being loved? Why am I this unworthy to love another?

His vision is blurred by tears. He falls to the floor, curling up into a ball on his side as he cries ever harder. Now just loud enough to become audible to any hidden onlookers. The whimpered moans of a defeated beasts. His body shakes with tremors of the agony erupting out of every pore. He is drowning again. Helplessly immobilized by his own mind.

Just stop being so fucking depressed you FUCKING LOSER! It a good thing they all left. They would only pity and despise the groveling grub which lays here! You would end it if only you had the stomach for it, you god damn coward! I hope I fight someone soon who I cannot beat. When I lose that battle, I just want them to end it, put me out of this misery. He slowly stands up to blow his nose, a momentary reprieve. A surface breath against the flailing drowning state he is in. He makes it all of a foot from where he stands before he falls to his knees. His body suddenly becoming immensely heavy. The brief breath passes in less than an instant.

Get up. Come on! Get up damn you! As if in protest to his commands to stand up his limbs grow even heavier and he falls face forward into the carpet. His thoughts go blank. Nothing more than deafening white noise. A burning white flame that burns away any and all thoughts. It is a terrible feeling which he has never been able to properly explain. It is as the someone has turned the volume from 5 to 11 and all that's playing is the feedback from the speakers themselves. This static drowns the rest of the world out around as he struggles to regain control of his mind. The rise and fall of his chest become more rapid and sporadic as he begins hyperventilating.

Breath! Just breath!

These commands are once again ignored. His mind goes blank again as his muscles begin writhing in mentally induced agony. His arms go from tightening to stretching outward then to holding his throat and chest as he now feels as though he cannot breathe. His legs similarly tighten and relax cause his back too arch.

After what feels like an eternity of despair and infinite agony, he is able to breathe again. He lays there for several minutes waiting to adjust to the newly lowered heart rate. After he is confident that he can in fact breath again he shifts his focus. He slowly, yet every so excruciatingly raises himself, using the furniture to helps lift himself up and stabilize. Still panting he stands with both hands gripping the edge of the sink so hard his knuckles turn stark white. His hold on the sink is the only thing keeping him standing. He stares into his reflection as the attack seems to subside. His body feels like he has just participated in a Triathlon. These attacks had a habit of draining all his energy both mentally and physically.

"I think… I think this ***one*** might have finally ended." He huffs out under his breath to no one aside from himself in the otherwise vacant room.

This unfortunately happens many nights when he is awake for a few hours longer than normal. They are always worse on nights like this when he lays alone. The massive amount of alcohol he has drunk tonight only make him more susceptible to these episodes. He collapses on his bed, all the energy drained out him. He is so empty at this point that he doesn't notice the door now cracked open and widening. Its Jill. She peaks her head out from the doorway to check on her old friend. He still doesn't register her presence. How could he? He is still huddled in the fetal position on his side facing the wall, back to the door. He faintly hears her soft footsteps close the distance between the door and the bed. She seats herself so delicately on the edge of the bed and places a hand in his hip in an attempt to comfort him. He flinches away from her touch, at first believing it to be more of his inner demons. Ghosts from his past that have come to take their revenge.

"Dillon" she calls out in the gentlest voice she has. "What's wrong darling? What has you so out of it?" Dillon stirs, eyes now open, as he realizes there is in fact another person in the room. He slowly sits up and maneuvers to face her, never making eye contact. "Hey there Dillon." She says as she brings one hand up and rest it on his cheek. The tears that continue to come pool at the top of her hand before flowing over and running down her arm, leaving a cold trail behind. "Oh, Dillon what's wrong?" she pleads, sounding close to tears herself. She is destroyed seeing her friend like this. The water works pick up volume and speed as he prepares to answer this question and spirals back down the rabbit hole.

"I, I am completely alone Jill." He cries out, his voice is felt bouncing back at them from every corner of the room. The vulnerability and despair in his voice is so intense that the others can physically feel the weight of the words he cries out. "I do not remember a time when I did not feel this hollowness inside. Even as a child I knew I was on the outside looking in. A floater. Never anchored to one group or place." He pauses to heave as he tries to catch his breath which is so quickly getting away from him. The other three have quietly assembled outside the door. Neither Jill nor Dillon know they have an audience. The spectators sit against the wall on either side of the door, that sunken empathetic feeling plagues them all as they attempt to empathize with Dillon.

Kirtland D. Neal

"All the people who I held dear, I soon realized were only in my life for these small fleeting moments. Many left me, seeing something I could not. I can't say I blame them since regardless of what I manage to accomplish I still hate myself to my core. I don't think I will ever be able to put that self-loathing into words so that others may understand me. Then, a good number of people I left be it my choice or by uncontrollable circumstances. As it was put in some old movie, 'single serving friends. Then there are the very precious minority, those people who light up your life with their sheer presence. A full moon in a darkened sky. Those beacons of spectacular light suffered the worst fate of all. They got close to me, too close for their own good. They signed their death sentences by getting so close to me. I am the dying star in a desolate system. Everything in my reach dies. So rather than destroy any more people, I built these walls. Walls so high you can't see the sun rise for miles upon miles on either side. I conceal myself within this labyrinth." He is now sitting all the way up and pounding his fist against his chest in agony. Jill and the others have begun to cry as they see how much he is suffering. "I hide behind my feigned narcissism and cockiness. The elegant mansion walls which conceal the lord in the depths of his estate. I always say I am ok. I cannot recall the last time that wasn't a lie. I feel alone even around my family. They love me I know. And some part of me loves them as well. Yet I am still but a stranger to them, someone they feel obliged to love and care about due to blood bonds." He now stares at her, unflinching as he admits many things out loud for the first time that he normally only tells himself internally. "Over these many years I have tried to hold them together to find meaning. But I eventually realized I had outlived my usefulness for that role. I slowly soured with this solitary existence. Withering flowers nobody feels like throwing out due to sheer laziness. I was too weak to simply die so I adapted. I grew cold and angry. I have done my best to suppress my feelings, growing numb to emotional and physical contact. Pretty soon when I had driven far enough along in my life, I pulled over to look around and saw that I stood alone on a dark and vacant pot hole riddled highway and was left to disrepair. I could never turn around." Dillon now stares at the foot of the bed as he rambles on. Essentially on autopilot as so much information spills out. Information he never intended to say out loud. "I try to dull the pain with alcohol, drugs, meaningless one-night stands, and anything to get my adrenaline pumping. Nothing I do changes these feelings, only putting off the misery. I don't know why I am so broken and damaged!" He wails as he relapses back into wordless sobbing, falling into Jill's arms. She doesn't know what to say so she just holds her friend as he weeps. She holds him hard against her chest as she tries to comfort him. They stay locked in this embrace for ages until Jill thinks of something that might rally Dillon back to his normal self.

"Do you remember what you had said to me and Thad when we brought Sonia home?" she asks rhetorically, "You held that small baby in your arms and looked at Thad and I and made us promise you something. 'You two have this wonderful little person here. She is so full of potential and possibilities, she can be anything she wants. She will be the most beautiful and amazing person we have ever met. You have to show her that the world owes her nothing, yet it can give her everything if only she has the drive and will power to go out and earn it. Remind her every single day that she has the ability to be smarter than anyone to come before her, more accomplished than us. I want this little niece of mine to become the most brilliant person yet. No matter what happens or comes at her way she will never be alone. Even should something terrible happen to you two she will have me.' You were the one who made us promise to tell her that she would never be alone. That goes both ways Dillon. As long as we are here, you are never ever going to be alone." He raises his head as the tears stop flowing. He begins to perk back up as he is reminded of a promise, he had them make so many years ago. Her soothing voice makes him feel even better as she talks. Before long he is back too normal. Standing up to wash his face he finds he is able to stand easily on his own for the first time in the last half hour. He spends a few minutes splashing his face with water over and over.

"Thanks Jill." Dillon says as he turns and wraps her in a massive hug. "I don't know what I would do with you." Dillon looks at his watch again. 0430. "I think I'm going to try and get a little bit of sleep before everyone wakes up. Thank you again Jill."

"It is really no problem Dillon." She replies as they separate, and she heads for the door. "If you ever want my help with one of these attacks let me know. Enjoy your sleep." She turns out the light as she closes the door behind her. Dillon gets into bed for the few fleeting hours of sleep he was accustomed to by now.

Jill pretends not to notice the others scurrying off to their perspective rooms as she exits Dillon's room. She can already tell there would be plenty of questions to answer in the morning. She barely makes it two steps before she hears doors slamming shut as the eavesdroppers disappear into their corners of the old building.

Chapter 14

January 20th, 2030

Two weeks of hell on Earth

Tampa, Florida

Liz Taylor

Liz slowly opens her eyes as she wakes up. Every ounce of her being is screaming out in pain. She hasn't even started to move yet. Liz spends the better part of twenty minutes laying perfectly still in the bed. During this immobility she is trying to recap everything from yesterday. Dillon had spent about an hour teaching them all how to use, clean and take care of the arsenal he had somehow acquired over the years. Most of which she and the rest of the group were fairly sure are illegal to have in the states. He had even more surprisingly managed to hide the armory in his beast of a truck. He had them all work with unloaded weapons for that first hour. They disassembled and reassembled the guns over and over again. He claimed they would have enough muscle memory to disassemble the guns all the way down to firing pins.

He gave them some bullets to work on marksmanship on the roof, as they one by one seemed to earn his stamp of approval for taking care of the weapons. They were aiming at targets that seemed to have been magically setup on the rooftop across the street and some more on street below. After everything was said and done, they had exhausted three hours on firearms. This included collecting the brass that was left and the cleaning of the guns one final time. Frank had muttered how the rifle he was using was cleaner than his own kitchen as Dillon told him to clean it again for the hundredth time. Dillon was proud of his toys.

Dillon had retreated to the garage to, as he put it "continue his conversation with Tommy". No one stopped him to ask more. During the following hour they had cooked some food for all of them, making sure not to disturb him and just go upstairs to eat so they could talk without having to yell over the loud music. The floor separating the two floors was soundproof so Thad's family could sleep even as a brawl broke out before last call. Dillon came up after another hour or so to grab the group. He then spent roughly three more hours training everyone on some hand to hand fighting and using the countless handheld weapons he seemed to have tucked away. Maybe "training" was not the right word, it was more like a montage of Dillon tossing people to the ground or drop kicking them into a wall.

Seriously though, where did this guy find yet alone store all of these weapons. He could have easily armed a small army with everything he had. Jill was the only who had appeared either unsurprised or unfazed by him having as much as he did. They only stopped training when they did because everyone was struggling to walk let alone spar. Everyone that is, except for Dillon who was tackling the tiresome effort of training everyone one on one as though it were his morning warm up. He helped everyone stretch out to avoid too much recovery pain. Everyone showered and went to bed as Dillon had offered to take the first guard shift. No one had the strength to argue. Jill and Sonia went up to their apartment upstairs as Frank and Liz each claimed their own room in the hallway of endless bedrooms.

Liz is staring blankly at the vandalized walls of the room while she tries to convince her muscles to move so she can get something to eat. After a long stretch of time with no results it proves to be her need to pee that gets her up first. Her entire body does so in stiff protest to her actions from the previous night. She gets dressed in yellow sundress that is several inches too short yet form fitting from the waist up. She throws on a pair of old blue jeans that are just starting to fray around the knees like old pants do. They are held up by a simple brown leather belt which is hidden under the bottom frills of the sundress. She still has the black high-top converse she had with her when Dillon had rescued her. She can't help but to think about that day as she puts the sneakers on. It seems like a lifetime ago, yet when she takes the time to think about how many days it's actually been its more like only a few weeks. When she stands up from the bed, she catches a glimpse of herself in the mirror. The new her is barely recognizable now even though she is still physically the same. Her entire body language has changed from the relaxed slouch she had always had to a more upright and strong appearance. Her eyes themselves seem to be tougher, no longer reflecting the frailty which she had always hated seeing in herself. Fashion wise her look left something to be desired. Dillon's exes were clearly either shorter or just more accustomed to skimpier outfits than she was. But despite her difference in taste she could work with it.

She makes her way to the bar area where Jill is sitting eating some breakfast, rifle leaning against her chair. She nods and smiles at Liz with a mouthful of food as Liz approaches the bar.

Kirtland D. Neal

"So how did you sleep in our drunk bunks?" Jill asks Liz after she washes down her mouthful of food with some coffee.

"The drunk what?" Liz starts before she understands what Jill is talking about, "Oh. Do you mean the hallway of random rooms? Yeah I slept fine."

"We call them many names." Jill giggles as she usually does whenever she got to explain the rooms to someone for the first time. "My husband, Thad, had wanted to make space for anyone that was too drunk to get home to have a spot to sleep comfortably. Hence the nickname Drunk bunks." There is a shimmer of sadness rooted in uncertainty that runs across her face when she mentions her husband's name. Liz pretends not to notice. She likes Jill and doesn't want to dredge up any unpleasant topics if they could be avoided. So, trying to change the topic to something a bit less emotional she figures she might press her luck and try to get some answers she so desperately desires.

"So… How long have you known Dillon?" Liz prods in that small voice children often use when they are expecting to get snapped at for something they say. Jill's face does not harden with anger like Liz had feared. Jill's expression is surprisingly soft with a sad looking sort of kindness. Her light pink lips subtly curve to form the faintest and most gentle smile. The small change of emotion resembles the way an elderly person would look upon remembering things from their youth. This newly adopted attitude shocks Liz at first. She doesn't expect to ever see such kindness on anyone's face after the world sank into the hell where they now live. Liz feels like a normal person for the briefest of moments.

"Many years ago, Dillon and Thad were once classmates. More years have passed since then than either would like to admit." Her smile grows the way one does when making a well-meaning joke about a loved one. "In fact, Dillon is the reason

Thad and I met in the first place. Him and I became friends after he began dating one of my best friends in high school. Isabella Pagan. We were neighbors for many years after her parents had moved there from San Juan, Puerto Rico. You should have seen how surprised everyone was when this scrawny little white boy walks up to Izzy and starts speaking almost perfect Spanish. The sneaky bastard had never told any of them that English was in fact his second language. His family had lived in like Spain or somewhere like that for a few years when he was younger." Jill has to pause for a moment as she laughs at the memory.

"Anyways, him and Isabella had been dating for a few months of, I think it was about junior year. A group of us had snuck out to go to the Gasparilla night parade that year. The night parade was always the last part of the Gasparilla celebration which happened every year to celebrate some pirate invasion that had happened so long ago. The night parade was also primarily for adults only, so we had to make sure our parents were not going to avoid getting caught. We decided to get some food at Hamburger Mary's after the parade had ended. As we were walking back to our cars afterwards, I realized I didn't have my phone. Since I had last seen it at the restaurant I decided to check there. I told the group to go on without and that I would catch up in a few minutes." Jill begins shaking her head a little as her eyes grew dark with self-chastisement.

Liz catches sight of a shadow lurking in a nearby doorway over Jill's shoulder. Its Frank. Silently listening to the story, not wanting to interrupt as he too wants to know more about Dillon. His true motives differ somewhat from what Liz expects them to be. He simply winks at Liz and puts a finger to his lips. Liz doesn't say anything and just returns her focus to Jill before she notices the eavesdropper.

Kirtland D. Neal

"I should have never gone back by myself. I was very thoughtless and oblivious to any of the nastiness in others back then." Jill berates her younger self.   "I got my phone easy enough, no trouble there. I had left it in the booth and the waiter had found after we walked out but couldn't find us outside, so he gave it to the host to hold on to in case we returned."

"I felt uneasy the second I walked back out on the street. It was maybe three in the morning, and the usually packed plaza was now vacant. I walked briskly back to where the cars had been parked earlier in the evening. The entire trip back I felt uneasy. Like I was being watched. I was maybe, halfway back to where I had left the group when it happened. Someone behind me forced me to detour into a dark alley. The attacker wrenched my shoulders in a U-turn type motion so that my nose slammed into the wall. I think I screamed. Or rather, I attempted to scream. I remember opening my mouth to scream, only it wasn't the sound it should have made. There was something hard and pointed pressed into the center of my back. A knife I think, never stopped to ask." Jill accidentally lets an awkward and nervous laugh escape her lips prior to recomposing herself and continuing the story. "Another shadowy figure stepped next to me as the one with the knife to my back stayed silently behind me. The side man told me to hand over my money and the same phone I had just gone back for. I looked down as my quivering hands reached for everything he wanted. Then I felt something impact the men mugging me. The knife was suddenly no longer pressed against my back. The guy behind me hits the floor like a bag of rocks and I look up to see Dillon slamming the second man to the ground. He holds the man up by his collar. This would be mugger is then rendered speechless as punches assault his face over and over again. It was many blows after the man goes limp before I had recollected myself enough to call out to Dillon. He looked up startled. The same look a dog gets when a noise gets his attention while he is eating. A cocktail of confusion, impatience, and agitation. There was a light spray of blood on his face and knuckles that scared me for second."

"I later found out that Isabella had felt uneasy when I wasn't back as fast, she would have liked so she asked him to come find me. He asked me not to say anything to the others as he walked to a nearby gas station bathroom and washed the blood off. I don't think I stopped shaking until I heard the voices of the group mingling around the cars. I never did say anything to them. But from that day Dillon and I have been close friends. I've spent all this time trying to somehow repay him for that moment of private heroism. The list of reasons I have to be thankful for him in my life only seems to keep growing as time ticks away. I barely manage to help him when he wakes in a frenzied state similar to the one you all saw him in last night. Even then it still feels insignificant."

"Shortly after that night he introduced me to Thad. After Dillon went off to the military it was mostly just me and Thad. About a year after we had graduated, we started dating. The rest as they say, is history." Jill smiles brightly as the fond memories of the last twenty or so years come flooding back to her. Liz can't believe it. Even at such an early age this man was helping others who needed him. The military part is no surprise given his treasure trove of weapons and equipment as well as his general way of moving around. This also makes her wonder when and why he had learned to fight like an animal.

"So then, Dillon has always been this well, intimidating?" Liz presses further. Jill does not seem to mind. It seems she rather enjoys talking about her old friend.

"For as long as I have known him, Dillon has always had this presence to him. Mostly he has been a sarcastic and charismatic man who goes out of his way to take care of others, even if it's just to make them smile. However, should someone threaten those close to him, then may god have mercy on their soul. Dillon is wired much in the same way that a guard dog is. He is loyal, loveable, and caring to those he protects, but will not hesitate to end anyone or anything that threatens his pack. It's one of the many reasons why people seem to gravitate towards him. He is the most protective creature I have ever met. That is one of the many reasons why he has been made a godfather to all the kids of his friends and brothers. We all know that should anything happen to us he will protect our children."

"Wow, I had no idea." Liz replies, even more shocked than before. She is starting to feel slightly ashamed of herself for how she had been judging this man during these many long weeks. "I have seen the protectiveness in plenty. It's just that the loveable and caring part seems to be very…um… lacking from the man I've seen so far. Did something happen or has he always been this… cold?"

Jill lets out a long sigh before answering, "Even when we were younger there was a sadness to him. It did not matter what his mood of the moment was, you could always see the shimmer of sadness in those smoky baby blues of his if you looked long enough. One of those people born with an old soul, I guess. I once asked his brother Tyler about that look in his eyes. I figured since Tyler was only 19 months younger than Dillon he would know if anyone would. He gave me almost the same response I have just given you. For as long as Tyler can remember his older brother has carried some heavy demons which only show in his eyes or the rare occasion where he loses control of his emotions. He does a rather good job of adopting a softer tone in his eyes so that people would never pry too much for no reason."

"In regard to the actual question of did something happen. Yes. Many misfortunes have befallen my dear friend over his lifetime, and that's just counting the few tragedies that I know of. He had a wife and child at one point." This news hit Liz like a sledgehammer to the chest causing her to lean back against the wall for support.

"When you say he *had* a wife and child, do you mean…?" Liz couldn't bring herself to finish her question, already fearing the response but needing to know. Jill gave a solemn nod to the inquiry.

"He met Veronica at a summer camp when he was 16 years old. She was a few years older than him at the time. They used to lifeguard together. They dated the second summer and ended up breaking up because of distance reasons. After we had graduated, she moved from Scotland to be with him and they got married shortly after. They had their son, Jason, about a year after Dillon joined the military. Those two were the only ones that I have ever seen diminish, and at times almost eliminate, the sadness he wears." The smile on Jill's face now traded places with a look of absolute pity.

"One stormy summer night however, he stayed late at work to help some of the guys getting ready to deploy. That's when it happened. It was storming hard that night and she wanted to bring him some dinner and see him, even if only for a few fleeting minutes. She brought their 2 years-old son Jason along since there was no one to watch him. Plus, he seemed to brighten up everyone's day when he visited Dillon at work. They were somehow that seemingly perfect little family, even for as short as that was. She showed up with some of her homemade lasagna, one of his favorites. The three of them sat there enjoying themselves as they ate. She always made extra so the other guys could eat with them. Her bank teller job was the only way they managed this kind of generosity on his Senior Airman salary on a consistent basis. After about twenty-five minutes she took little Jason home to put him to bed."

"The storm only seemed to get worse as the night went on. A drunk driver drifted into their lane and hit them head on over the bridge. Veronica and Jason were sent to the bottom of the bay as the car broke through the cement barrier and into the water. The other driver was sent flying through the windshield of his car and skipped across the pavement. He was dead upon initial impact. Veronica wasn't able to take her seatbelt off. The scuba divers found her holding her child so tightly that not even the coroner was able to separate them." Tears of old pain begin to trickle down her face as she recalls the tragedy.

"Dillon was so devastated. He buried them together as they should have been. But I don't think he has let himself get close to anyone the same way since that night. He…he seems to keep everyone he meets now at arm length. He told Thad once it's easier that way." The tears have stopped coming now. They briefly turn as they hear the now familiar sound of the speaker blasting music from the garage.

"Guess he is back in there to *talk* to Tommy some more. I almost feel sorry for the dumb kid." Jill says more to herself as she turns back to Liz.

"Why do you feel sorry for Tommy?" Liz asks innocently.

"Like I said Dillon protects his pack. That includes me and my Sonia. Tommy came after us to get to Thad, one of Dillon's oldest friends. Odds are Tommy has already begun to regret that decision. He was harsh when he saved me from those muggers all those years ago. That protective instinct coupled with whatever darkness found and changed him overseas spells trouble for anyone who crosses that line. I am confident those experiences sharpened the blunt object of rage into something far more frightening. He will always look after us though." She proclaims with a grin. "For better or worse, we are the closest thing to family he has left right now."

"Oh." She replies, eyes wide with realization.

"Yeah." Jill says flatly. "As I was explaining as far as Dillon goes though, there are few more major events that I have seen change him. His mom died a few short months after Veronica and Jason. That was an impossible year for that man. I wouldn't wish that year upon anyone."

"About four years later the war in Syria really heated up. After the Allied Annihilation in March of 2018 they put together a big joint branch command. He was one of the first ones to volunteer for the new joint force to go fight."

Even though the music continues she still checks around before carrying on. "I think a large part of him was hoping not to come back from Syria. He had so much anger and resentment inside of him and he saw the war as a useful way to release it. He was in charge of a small unit over there. From everything I have heard he seemed to have led it well. They were over there for roughly eight months without losing anyone. Then… then they got word of a big meeting of some important people and his group was tasked with slipping in to check and potentially clean up any complications." Jill stops as she mentally mulls something over. The gears visibly turning behind those milk chocolate eyes of hers.

"All the war stuff I mostly know from what his dad passed on. Only a select few of his oldest and closest friends were told. This included Thad and I. Needless to say you should under no circumstances bring any of what I am telling you up to him. Got it?" Liz nodded. She was already too afraid to even imagine talking to Dillon about any of this.

Kirtland D. Neal

"Good. Well, apparently, the whole meeting was a setup. They were fed bad intel somewhere along the line. It was an ambush. An absolute slaughter. Out of the hundred or so men in the unit, less than 10 survived the massacre. Dillon and a half dozen other men from his unit were taken hostage. After several months of no contact for ransom or anything they were all considered killed in action. We were all told after the search had proven fruitless. Nobody could believe it. Even back then he seemed invincible." Jill seems to get cold as she shudders before wrapping her arms around herself. Sonia shows up to hug her mom from under Jill's arms and squeezing tight. An appreciative smile spreads across Jill's face.

"Thanks baby. I didn't realize you were there. How long have you been listening? I don't want you to hear this horrific story."

"No problem momma. And don't worry, dad told me all this over the years. Usually when he would get so drunk that he forgets what he told me the next morning. They were uncommon nights, but they happened enough for me to have heard most of this a few times over by now." Sonia sheepishly responded, knowing how much trouble he would be in if they saw him again. An angry grin spreads across Jill's face.

"I am going to kill your father next time I see him." Jill fumes for a moment before carrying on.

"We held a celebration of life for Dillon. He wanted everyone to party, drink, dance and laugh at his funeral. He hated the depressingly awkward atmosphere of normal funerals. I have never seen any of those guys that bad when they got drunk before. For the first time I saw a fragment of Dillon's sadness in their eyes. Yet even if the sadness in the eyes of the dozens of people who showed up, their collective anguish still paled in comparison to the blinding sorrow that occasionally shone through Dillon's eyes. We put a headstone for him next to Verona's and Jason's.

Apocalypse Virus: Initial Infection

Some two or three years after the funeral he managed to return.
He just showed up at his dad's place one day out of the blue."

"Ricci, one of his old roommates and closest friends, was
still in at the time. He was over in the region and a key component
in coordinating missions from the operating command of the
middle east. They received an odd e-mail from an unknown
account. The sender claimed to be one of the hostages taken a few
years before. The VPN had been bounced around making it
practically impossible to locate the origin of the message. No one
there believed it at first, or rather no one trusted it to be anything
besides a trap. None of them could find the energy to hope for that
impossibility in the face of the crushing despair they had felt a
few years prior when the team was massacred. They must have
spent almost ten days debating what to do before they decided to
send a rescue team. They sent the most experienced special
operators they had at their disposal."

"A strike force consisting of two dozen men was sent to
the site the e-mail had described. Ricci and the rest of the
coordinating team watch from back at base thanks to the body and
helmet cams the team wore. The team took their time to scope out
the location for a while before moving in. They didn't see any
movement or activity for roughly three hours, so they deemed it
safe enough to move in. When they rolled up, they found Dillon
was actually alive. He was a little malnourished and riddled with
scars but still in some decent shape. Ricci said he still had a hard
time recognizing his old friend even in person back at base. They
found him sitting at a blood splattered table eating some slop he
had managed to cook from what was left. All his captors were
dead and burned in a massive charred pile outside. There was
nothing left but brittle blackened bones, cold for days by now.
They were surprised that he had somehow managed to escape and
kill his jailers, especially after all this time and given his physical

condition. Scars had now riddled his body a few times over."

"He told the team that there had been some scientist doctor types that had put him on a slab many times. They had left before he got the chance to kill them too. He seemed more disappointed about them escaping than angry. Most of the people watching through the live feed threw up when they saw the lab. Some of the guys on the team lost their lunches as well. It was worse than any horror movie they had ever seen. The metal slab looked like it had been taken from a funeral home, the ones they embalm people on. This one however had terminals welded on that were hooked up to several car batteries. Rust dotted the edges of the table. The tools scattered on and around the table were just as dirty, many were new to the men. Traces of several different liquid compounds were covering many of the tools. Ricci said it was more terrifying than any of the sci-fi horror movies. It was worse because this was real life. They couldn't believe what they found. They also recovered confusing records and plans for various experiments and test subjects. Plans which highlighted Dillon's physical and medical information baffled even some top medical doctors, both private and military."

"It was when Dillon returned from this that he seemed to have evolved to the cold and unflinching individual he is now. He was no longer the man we had all grown to love. He spent a few months at home to recover before returning to the military. He still didn't seem to realize he was actually here for the first two months. He slammed some douche bag against the wall right here in the bar. Guy was bad mouthing the military even after Thad had told him to stop. One of those people who had a chip on their shoulder and either couldn't join or got kicked out during training so suddenly the military was the big bad to them. Dillon was up and across the bar before anyone else noticed, he asked the guy to talk about something else. The guy told Dillon to go fuck himself. A moment later he wasn't able to say anything because Dillon lifted the man up by his throat. He corrected the man for his rudeness before slamming him down to the ground. You can see a slight indentation in the floor right there." She points at a sunken area in the center of the horseshoe.

"He had a lot of friends with him that night as it turned out. That was the biggest brawl I have ever seen here." She pauses, sipping her coffee as her eyes glass over for a second as she relives that fight.

"Dillon had immediately yelled at anyone who tried to join in on his side. Warning them that this was his fight, and his alone. That man was the only one still standing in the end, not unscathed but still standing. Thad was both scared and impressed by his old friend. Him and everyone else who witnessed that beating that night. Nobody around here made the mistake of talking bad about the military after that. That was back when this place was still relatively young in her years as a bar."

Jill pats one of the old support beams running up through the bar. The creeping light of the rising sun has begun to penetrate the gorgeous windows, causing all of them to squint ever more so.

"That about sums up the major reason he is how he is now. At least as far as I know of. There are still many things I don't know about what's happened in his life over the years. Now, before you ask any more questions let's get some food in you. You must be starving." Jill finishes as her and Sonia turn and walk towards the kitchen. Liz and Frank both stand there silently. Neither one knowing how to feel having learned all of this about Dillon. One fact hits Liz immediately though. She is hungrier than she remembered being in an awfully long time.

Chapter 15

January 20th, 2030

Tampa, Florida

Dillon Thompson

The damage that Dillon had done to Tommy yesterday doesn't look so bad this morning. Dillon washes off the excess clotted blood and cleans it up a little bit before checking on Tommy himself. He extends two fingers to his neck. A few long moments pass by unnoticed. Tommy slowly begins to stir as Dillon cleans him up and checks his pulse.

Yup, still alive. Dillon thinks to himself, a little too nonchalantly.

The black bag is ripped off Tommy's head causing him to wince as the bright light behind Dillon is blinding. Dried sweat and grime have left filthy streaks across his face. Once he acclimates to the sudden brightness, he becomes wide eyed with fear, his eyes are darting all around the room until they finally center in on Dillon, standing in front of him. He attempts to cower away from his interrogator, a fruitless effort given the restraints holding him to the chair. Dillon removes the headphones and places the player on the charger.

"If I remove the gag are you going to scream or be loud?" Dillon ask his captive audience. He is answered with a vigorous head motion that's so intense it shakes the chair itself. "Alright. Are we going to be a bit more helpful today than yesterday?" This response is far less likely than the previous one. Content, yet disappointed with the apparently genuine reply Dillon removes the gag from Tommy's mouth, letting it hang around his neck. Tommy begins to open and close his mouth while licking the inside of his dry mouth. Dillon grabs the bottle of water with a straw and brings it to the boy. Tommy greedily sucks up all of the water within a few minutes. He is still thirsty and incredibly hungry. The room reeks of blood, sweat, and urine. Tommy had seen no chance of him getting a bathroom break early on in this little adventure the two of them had departed on and decided to not even bother holding it.

"So where is Alex holed up at? And why does he want Thad?"

"He has managed to take the fair grounds. The majority of his people stay around either the event center where they normally hold the graduations or the pioneer village. He tries to keep the more unhinged people over at the village to hide them out of sight until he needs them. Some of us call it his Psycho Kennel."

"I honestly have no idea why he wants Thad. He has been sending us out to pick up certain people that he wants. Some of them it's obvious why we grab them, others are seemingly random. We grabbed some of the doctors from one of the hospitals a few days after we set up there. There's something different about him now." He suddenly falls silent. Tommy's gaze slips to the ground as his face changes to something Dillon finds surprising. It almost looks sad but there is a layer of fear. Like a person remembering a tragic event they wish they could have stopped.

"Alex, I mean." The tone of Tommy's voice shifts. Dillon can't exactly place it. Somewhere between despair and anger. "He is not the same guy he was before all this. The gang leader he used to be seems to be gone but not dead. Morphed, no… evolved… into something darker… more… sinister. He is screening anyone that wants to come there for safety. It's not good man, but I need to survive. I cannot die!" By this point Tommy has rapidly grown hysterical, tears rushing down his face. His voice now grows muffled by the sounds of his own sobs. Dillon has to lean in closer in order to discern what the emotionally distraught man is saying.

"He promised to let my mom and sister stay there if I helped him. He has made similar agreements with the majority of the guys we use to run with. Only thing is, once he lets people in, he holds them as leverage against us in order to force us to carry out his orders, no matter how fucked up and deranged they may be. We have decided we can live with our sins if it means keeping our families safe"

Dillon stands straight upon hearing this news. This is worse than anything he could have imagined. What the fuck is going on over at the fairgrounds? And how is Dillon supposed to move forward from here? What should he do with Tommy? As these snowballing problems swarm Dillon, a crazy idea begins to form in his head. Is it crazy? Or maybe it is incredibly brilliant. He quickly weighs the odds before advancing. The odds are nowhere near favorable, but it is something. This half-baked plan is equal parts insanity and genius. This psychotic plan is more than the nothing he had prior to this morning.

Apocalypse Virus: Initial Infection

"Tommy." Dillon calmly says as he places a hand his shoulder. The young man stops talking and looks up with uncertainty, unable to read Dillon's expression. Dillon has adopted a much gentler tone as he presses his luck a little more.

"If I can get your mom and sister out and set up a safe place for you guys and do as you want. If I can do that, will you promise to go back to being the same guy I knew before everything went to shit?"

"I can't risk losing any more of my family. I'm sorry." He instantly replies.

"I haven't even told you what all I need from you yet. Do you think my success would be that impossible?" Tommy nods, unable to look him in the face. Dillon lets out a disappointed sigh before he replaces the gag in Tommy's mouth. Dillon turns the music up again as he contemplates what games he should play with the boy first. Tommy initially thinks this is all some sick joke. The disdain on his face makes this evident. How can someone return to who they were after dealing with this hellish world? Or even just simply enduring the personalized hell Dillon has orchestrated? He can't bet the lives of his remaining family on one man against an army, regardless of who it is.

Dillon spends most of the day water boarding Tommy, only stopping to refill the bucket. He still sees the same reluctant resolve in Tommy's eyes at the end of their day together. Dillon doesn't even waste his breathe on asking a question he already knows the answer too. Tommy is still shivering as Dillon reapplies the headset and hood. He douses yesterday's reopened wounds in alcohol. Soliciting a long drawn out muffled wail. Dillon returns the bag and headphones to Tommy's head before he shuts off the stereo and returns to train everyone else some more.

They keep in this little routine for another week. Each day something new and painful. That same defiant and stubborn look in his eyes is still there, day after day. He begs and pleads for Dillon to stop with desperate looks in his eyes which dances with the defiance. Even throughout it all, this look of reluctant defiance never wavers. Dillon does electroshock the first day after the water boarding. A car battery is attached to a voltage dial with clamps going out. One is attached to a strip of metal in a kiddy pool with a few inches of water placed beneath Tommy. The other end is connected to simple old silver necklace that Dillon scavenged from Jill's jewelry box. He chose silver since it's the most conductive metal with a high thermal conductivity. Plus the image of the naked young man with a shiny all silver necklace is slightly comical to Dillon. Regardless of how many times Dillon shocks the young man his questions remain unanswered.   He spends the next two days straight making one square inch slices across Tommy's skin. Dillon makes the cuts in sets of five at a time before squeezing lemon juice and rubbing salt in the wounds. Taking his time with each motion to draw out the pain while minimalizing real damage. Each flick of the blade takes almost a minute each and is deeper than an average cut. Dillon makes it to the fifth or sixth round of slashes before his guest passes out the first time. Dillon wakes him up and repeats the process. Tommy passes out multiple times from pain during both of these days. Dillon decides to move on after he carves his way from wrists to shoulders.

Dillon leaves him alone the fourth day to try and avoid killing him. Tommy is given one cup of water a day and no food, just enough to keep him alive. The boy is starting to show signs of prolonged dehydration. No signs of starvation have started appearing yet.

The day after his day off, Dillon takes a glowing red-hot piece of rebar to close up all the open wounds on Tommy. He finishes the day off by making Tommy take several huffs of high concentration tear gas. The cleanup portion takes especially long this day. Seeing no change in the boy's determination Dillon presses on the next day, breaking every digit and limb with the help of a pair of pliers and his hammer. The straw that brakes the camel's back is scrubbing the soles of his hands and feet with steel wool and fiber glass until the surface of the skin is indiscernible from the blood. A zoomed in picture of the soles may have resembled ground beef in the past. The glimmer of determination has finally vanished from Tommy's eyes. Dillon knows he no longer has to hurt the poor bastard.

"I was being completely serious. I have never wanted you as an enemy, or a corpse. You are much more useful to me alive. This won't be leverage, just an act of good faith. I just want Alex. As long as you can walk me through on how to get in, I can promise to do everything in my power to bring them back alive." Dillon is able to make a rather persuasive argument even in spite of everything. Tommy sits there with his mouth hanging wide open. Dillon is fairly sure that has more to do with the dehydration, torture, starvation and general fatigue than anything he was saying.

"Understand this is about me stopping Alex now to keep Thad and his family safe as well as to stop whatever he is planning before it happens. Also, if you cross me or lead me into a trap or anything duplicitous like that, I will not hesitate to end you and your family."

The two men stay in a stare off for several long, silent minutes as Tommy makes up his mind on what to do.

"You would really rescue them and give us a safe place to stay if I let you at Alex?" A simple nod is the silent reply. "And if I don't help you?" Tommy desperately searches every avenue before choosing a path.

"I might just have to resume the path our previous *conversation* has been taking up until now." He lifts his head towards Tommy's wounds. "only this time it will be something more permanent than all the superficial damage I have done. I am going to be completely honest. I really don't enjoy treating people with this level of *hospitality* when they don't deserve it. And believe me, I don't believe that you deserve any of this, but my hands were forced." This helps to make Tommy's choice an easy one.

The next hour and a half is fairly easy on the two as they go back and forth in a little Q&A session. Throughout this discussion the pieces of Dillon's insane plan to get at Alex seem to come together. It is still roughly 80% suicidal, but history has taught Dillon to bet on himself. War and conflict are his matter of expertise.

Chapter 16

January 27th, 2030

Stinky Pete's, Tampa

Just over three weeks in hell

Everyone is shocked to see Dillon help Tommy walk out of the garage. They are even more horrified to see how much Tommy is visibly different from his brief time in the garage. Both physically and mentally speaking. He has his hands and feet heavily wrapped in gauze. He still winces with each and every step. The scars are still visible over the tank top and gym shorts Dillon had given him. Sonia grabs a trash can from behind the bar and throws up from the sight of him. Dillon walks Tommy over and sits him at the bar. Carried is more fitting description.

"You still drink screwdrivers like you use to?" Dillon asks as he walks behind the bar and ignores the horrified looks from the rest of the group.

"Yeah man, you're the one who got me hooked on those in the first place." Tommy croaks, sounding as though he is just coming to catch up with an old pal. He tries to smile but it is obviously forced and unauthentic. The fake smile immediately turns into a grimace of pain. Jill isn't all that surprised by what Dillon is capable of, she is however extremely surprised to see that Tommy had held out for as long as he had. She had heard stories from a few of the veterans who had come in over the years and recognized Dillon. Somehow even having heard these stories she never thought any less or any differently of Dillon. After seeing some of his handy work in person it only solidified her trust in her old friend. For Jill it is clear that as long as she has Dillon around that her and Sonia will be safe.

I have a plan to go after Alex and his people. I won't tell you guys the plan until I leave for it in, let's say two days. I will be of need of some things. I'll come up with a list and have you guys search around here and see what all we got before I go on supply runs." Dillon finishes as he pours six shots and hands them out after giving Tommy his screwdriver. Jill raises an eyebrow at Dillon when she realizes that the last shot is for Sonia. He simply smiles and hands it to Sonia while maintaining eye contact with Jill. He gives his old friend a devilish wink. Dillon figures with the way the world is now that girl will no longer have the luxury of being a child. On some level Jill picks up on what he is thinking and relaxes, never saying a word about it. He also remembers all of them drinking as early as freshman year of high school, so he knows it isn't the girl's first drink. They all wait a moment for Dillon to come up with a toast.

"To the ones we have lost, the one we don't know about, and the ones we hope to find. And to surviving." And with that they all raise their glasses together before downing the shots of tequila. Dillon didn't even think of handing out training wheels, he hadn't needed a lime or salt since he was 21. The faces around the room make it clear that none of them had ever been that way. He can't help but smile a little when he sees this. His smile alone seems to brighten up the room and put everyone else at ease.

Apocalypse Virus: Initial Infection

Within two days Dillon has turned the old bar into an easily defendable fort. He has the pleasure of running into several small groups of thugs during his supply runs. Jill never asks how he had gotten so much blood and dirt on himself for simple runs. No one does. They all know yet felt more comfortable turning a blind eye to it. He has proven many times over by now that he is more than capable when it came to fighting and surviving. Dillon writes down instruction for everyone each morning before he leaves on his run and hands them off to whoever has guard duty when he leaves. He usually returns around lunch to unload all that he has found and to grab a quick bite before quickly resuming his search. He makes around three to four trips a day at this pace. Once he is done for the day, he looks over the progress the others have made and edit what he thinks needs changing. They actually surprise him with how much they manage to accomplish.

As the sun rises and warms up the chilly Wednesday morning on Tampa Bay Dillon's plan is almost ready to begin. He calls everyone into Tommy's room since he is still to hurt too far go very without help. Tommy and Jill look on edge while the other three groggily gaze over at Dillon. All of them are anxiously awaiting the battle plan previously promised by the stoic man.

"Morning guys. So, first things first I am going to confront Alex and his people on my own. That is non-negotiable!" He raises an open hand to preemptively silence Jill's protest. "I plan to be gone at least two weeks, maybe more. While I am gone, I have a favor to ask of you all. I want you guys to search for Thad while I am gone. I am fairly certain that he hasn't been found yet since I've run into a few groups of thugs nearby. I think he might be over in Channel side. So, I want y'all to go search there, but there is a catch. Someone has to stay here to watch and tend to our guest." He adds with a nod towards Tommy. "So, I have picked the pairings I think would works best for scouting out Channel side and doing various runs while I am gone. Unfortunately, Jill and Sonia will have to alternate going out in order to make sure that Thad recognizes and trust at least one person in which ever group contacts him first. Jill, I think you should go with Frank which would leave Liz and Sonia as the other team. If you all feel the groups are better being swapped then feel free to work that out for yourselves while I am gone. I will hang his old lettermen in the window upstairs before I leave."

"What good will placing some old jacket in a window do?" Liz interrupts completely confused. It isn't Dillon who answers her question though.

"It's something those two used to do growing up after they had either been gone for a few days or had been grounded. It's their personal signal that basically says the coast is clear, you can come over." Jill can't help but to smile as she explains their little secret. Liz is almost positive she sees Dillon's cheeks redden a bit as Jill explains the significance of the jacket in the window. Dillon coughs, feeling a little weird.

"As I was saying, y'all are going to split up in the two teams and take turns searching for Thad around Channel side while the other team will keep this place safe and help take care of Tommy." Despite their expressions, everyone seems to be on board with everything so far. "If I am not back in a month, assume I am dead." Everyone else in the room shifts uncomfortably upon hearing this. None of them can find any words to say. Dillon lets that sink in for a few moments. 30 days seems like an eternity since the world pretty much shit the bed. That paired with the possibility of Dillon dying really threw everyone for a loop.

"I'm counting on you guys to find Thad while I am gone. I am confident you all will survive and hopefully thrive even without me. If I don't make it back by then, go to the harbor and take my boat to the island. I am going to roll out in an hour. I will be packing a bag and checking on shit here before then, should any of you want to say goodbye.

Chapter 17

22nd of December, 2029

STS Off Site

Tabitha

    Tabitha makes sure to quickly get redressed. She ties up and gags the sedated security guard. She downloads the security camera feed with the help of her trusty Doppelganger Box. This had been some of the hardest data to secure so far since the only place she could find the footage on site was here. Everything is backed up though at a regional server farm somewhere in Alabama. She checks to make sure that all the scientist and various other employees have gone home before proceeding to the Secured Storage room. Here she makes a rather shocking discovery. Her K-55 and the related research is there. That isn't what scares her the most. As she is taking pictures of her old notes, she begins to notice someone else's hand writing. She can't tell whose it is, but she is confident that if she is correctly understanding the changes then it would turn her cure all into an unstable bioweapon. There is a 12-digit designation towards the end of the corrections. 01022030-2359. She can't figure it out. In the moment so she will have to settle with the pictures. As Tabitha returns all the notes to their original order her hand bumps into a vile, she hadn't seen a moment ago. She holds the light on her phone up so she could read what it said. **Darkseid Serum, 5ᵗʰ Gen. Designation D-5. Anti-K Formula.** If this means what she thinks it does, then her worst fear has just been realized. They have already made at least 5 versions of the bioweapon. They have taken her research for a better world and turned it into something so phenomenally dark and twisted. She quickly swipes the vial.

Her entire body shakes with equal parts fear and rage as she rushes back to the security room. She undoes Tony's restraints before injecting him with something to gradually wake him like he is naturally waking up from a nap. It is once again time for her to utilize those years of Theatre Club in high school.

"Morning sleepy head." She giggles as she toys with his hair. He sits up slowly. Tony looks more disoriented than she had expected.

"What happened?" He inquires looking around, some details coming back to him, like the purpose of their little rendezvous. He slowly begins moving around trying to locate his stuff.

"You fell asleep while I was rubbing your back and checking to see if I had broken skin. Which I did in a few spots. Sorry."

"Fuck! Lana is going to kill me. How long was I out for?"

"Maybe 45 minutes, give or take. Just tell her that you had to stay late to supervise some of us nerds finishing up an experiment." She waits for him to finish pulling up his pants before she pulls him in close for a long goodbye kiss.

"I will see you after New Year's. I have to go get ready for my much needed vacation." She waves to him as she closes the door behind her.

Tabitha hurries her way out of the building as calmly as she can manage. She gets in her car and races home. The moment she puts the car in park outside of her apartment building she immediately breaks down in a panic induced hysteria. She can no longer hold back the swell of emotions churning inside of her.

The idle little Honda sucks down almost two gallons of gas by the time she wipes away the last tear, her eyes having dried out. Hopefully with all that out of her system now she can resolve herself to carry out her plan as coldly and calmly as possible.

Chapter 18

30 January 2030

Outside Stinky Pete's Bar, Tampa

Dillon

Everyone except for Tommy is out front saying goodbye to Dillon. Sonia is crying like she used to whenever he would have to leave again for work. She loves her Uncle Dillon more than she can express, he knows it and can't help but to shed a tear as he pulls himself from her hug. Even this crusty bastard has some soft spots left.

"You better not go dying on me old man. Who else is supposed to sneak me cool shit and scare any of the boys who bother me?" Sonia asks teary eyed. She holds out a hand with her pinky extended in the air. They do their signature pinky promise-handshake combo before drawing each other in for another fierce embrace.

"You can't get rid of me that easily, Super girl. Just hold down the fort for me alright." He teases before moving over to say goodbye to Jill and the others.

"We will find Thad. I found that man all those years ago. You just worry about taking those bastards out." Jill being ever the pragmatic mother bear. Dillon nods as he releases her from his hug. Frank can't really think of anything to say so he just gives a silent bro hug accompanied with a stern nod of unspoken understanding.

Liz is awkwardly shifting her weight from one foot to the other when Dillon finally steps in front of her. She suddenly freezes once she makes eye contact with him. After many long moments of awkward inaction, she manages to surprise Dillon, along with the other 3 in attendance. Liz leaps forward and plants a shockingly passionate kiss on his lips. His eyes became wider than hubcaps as they dart to the other to see if this is actually happening. Their unison expressions affirmed that this is in fact happening. She finally breaks away after what feels like an eternity to everyone else. Her cheeks are now beat red as she begins stumble for words.

"I…Um…I just wanted to, like thank you for saving my life that very first day and keeping me… and everyone else," she nervously motions to the rest of the group. "…for keeping all of us alive this whole time. Yeah, that's what that was for. It was my way of saying thanks." She spats out as though trying to convince herself more than him or the others. "Well…anyways… um…you should really make sure you come back in one piece. I don't know what I would…. I mean what we, I don't know what we would do without you. So please make it back here." Her big doe eyes close as she rushes in for an embrace so strong it makes it hard for Dillon to breath. Once she finally releases him, she shyly retreats a step or two, not able to look him in the eyes but smiling none the less.

"I…I will do my best to come back." Dillon is suddenly finding it hard to think clearly. An old part of him tells himself how he doesn't deserve to come back. He never should have made it back from Syria. Dillon's watch suddenly begins beeping.

He looks down to see that it is 0900. Time for him to finally roll out and make his way to what might very well be his death bed. "See y'all in a few weeks. Good luck and be safe." Upon finishing these unusual fair wells Dillon picks his back up and slings both straps over their perspective shoulders.

Once again looking like a modern day god of war Dillon begins his trek to the fairgrounds, making sure to utilize the smaller roads on either side of 21st street. Moving cautiously, he expects what was normally a 15-minutes' walk to Lake Avenue to take at least an hour maybe more if he runs into trouble.

Dillon stops around 1000 hours to take cover in a rundown building over by Mallory avenue and Banza street. He practically trips over a big ugly sign that read **A Perfect Start Academy**. He is trying to remember why the old building had been unoccupied for all these years before the functioning world shit the bed. He is sitting on top of a dust covered kid's table drinking water when he remembers a story that had played across the news reel one night several years back. STS, some big corporation that made and owned almost everything had bought out all the old places like this so that kids would go to their own programs in some big humanitarian/social effort to better educate the kids or some shit like that. From what he can remember, those bastards had been making a lot of big moves over the last decade. From what anyone could tell it had helped push the world forward by decades. Dillon couldn't help but to laugh as he sat there. *If you big brainy bastards were so smart, then why did all this happen?* He is absolutely certain that the lack of aid from anyone meant that this is at the very least a nationwide disaster. Something in his gut told him this surpassed any imaginary borders though. This was quite probably a worldwide phenomenon. He decides to search the building while he is here. There is mostly a bunch of art supplies and children's toys. The only things of use he manages to find are some rolls of duct tape and 4 of the little bottles of water. He pours two of them into his big bottle and tucks the rest away for later use.

He is halfway to the door when a noise from the back of the building catches his attention. Every muscle in his body tenses up, springs under immense pressure ready to snap into action. He raises his AR-15 before flicking the side mounted flashlight on. He slowly clears the decrepit building, everything seems fine. He is about to chalk it up to paranoia when movement in the backyard catches his attention through the window. One of those mutated monsters he had seen from his loft is sniffing around an old play set. It is far more gruesome up close. The creature is easily 8-feet tall while on all fours. It is nearly hairless, a fact which only increases the overly grotesque aesthetic of the beast. The eyes have grown to the diameter of tennis balls. Even in the brightness of the morning it's pupils still make up roughly two thirds of the ocular surface area. The pupils are noticeably blacker than a normal person's. The iris is absent all together. The Sclera, the part which is normally white on a person is a deep crimson. The nose has somehow become more canine in shape and appearance, protruding from its face an inch or so. This seems to have caused some of the skin to stretch and rip in places around this area. These exposed spots are swollen with a grotesque sheen to them. A clear indication of the numerous infections which have set in. The lips have receded, further exposing the blood-stained gums which make way for the enlarged canines which seem chipped in ways so that each is incredibly sharp. The head itself seems larger than normal, yet still looks small in proportion the rest of the massive form of the beast. The neck is both stockier and longer than it ought to be. Perhaps a foot or so from chin to where the collar bone is buried beneath an insane amount of muscle. Its shoulders are twice as wide as any lineman's in pro football. The front paws seem rather elongated while paw like. This hints at the possibility that they still hold some of the same uses as regular hands while also acting as anterior paws. The rest of the beast's trunk barely tapers down by the time it hits the engorged hips. It has massive thighs which turn into werewolf like haunches. Both rear paws are massive and deadly with their elongated claws. The destructive set of paws that were once hands appear even larger, each digit easily 6 to 8 inches long with talons extending another few inches. It's sickly gray leathery skin almost seems to shine in the sunlight.

It is one of the monsters which Dillon had come to refer to as Monster Mutts or just Mutts for short. He had noticed that there were a handful of different variations of monsters. He threw up the first time he saw someone change into one of these monsters. The process had started off much like someone having a seizure. An eternity of painful agony later they would go rigid as their skin and muscles bubbled and seemed to crawl around, gradually changing the person's physiology. The total time of transformation seemed to vary from ten minutes to almost an hour long from what he had observed so far.

The blood dried up on the mutt's claws and muzzle seemed to prove that it was as deadly as it seemed. This little observation gifted Dillon with the gruesome visual of this beast tearing into some freshly killed corpses. Dillon manages to slow down his breathing long enough to think calmly again. He flicks the flashlight off to avoid drawing its attention prematurely. He keeps the rifle trained on the mutt while rapidly throwing together a plan that he is positive will kill him. He can't help but to smile a little. He has always performed better under pressure with the odds stacked against him. It is for that reason that he is sure the plan will work. He doesn't want to wait for it to move on and risk other mutations showing up so that leaves him with the daunting task of killing the beast. He smoothly pulls out the silencer from the holder in his pack without moving his eyes away from the mutt. This is more of a reflexive muscle memory movement than anything actually planned. With the silencer securely equipped to the end of the barrel he switches from semi-automatic to fully automatic with a flick of his thumb. He makes his way to the back door, carefully avoiding all the debris on the ground. He slowly slides the glass door open, hoping that if he can avoid shattering the glass and keep this quit that he might avoid drawing anymore monsters to him. He gives a quick whistle. The way one would call the family dog. The mutt's eyes dart up to him with frightening speed. It doesn't have time to process anything as Dillon releases a barrage of bullets directly into those dark voids it has for eyes. It gives a low whine which sends a shiver down Dillon's back and leaving the hair standing in its wake. Dillon doesn't stop until his clip is emptied. He reloads so quick that it takes him a moment before he realizes that the mutt has collapsed. It seems far too easy for just that to have killed the creature.

He cautiously approaches the body. The sights of his rifle never straying from the target. He stops halfway to the monster as the behemoth staggers up to its original height. Blood pours forth from where its eyes used to be which only adds to the frightening ferocity of the creature. Evidently Dillon had only succeeded in blinding as well as thoroughly pissing it off. The mutt paws at its face as it tries to wipe the blood away in a useless attempt at clearing its vision. Upon the quick deduction that it will not be able to use its eyes the monster begins to sniff about in search of Dillon's scent. Dillon takes this moment to turn and haul ass. Dillon is maybe 20 feet down the street before the sound of the mutt crashing out the front door fills the air. His feet are pounding against the pavement faster and faster as the adrenaline takes over. His breathing is so rapid it feels as though a lung might pop out of his chest. He does not need to look back as he can hear the monstrosity closing the distance between them. Dillon's eyes dart left and right as he desperately searches for something to help him escape. The sound of the beast's panting is almost drowned by its claws scrapping along the asphalt. The monster is almost right on top of him.

Chapter 19

Streets of Tampa

Dillon

Dillon's last hope quickly takes the form of a narrow alley way between two of the buildings. The opening is just barely wide enough for him to dive through which should prevent the beast from following him. Or so he hopes. He turns and jumps into the narrow opening as the mutt's claws rip into his left calf. He lets out a wail of agony as his body slams into the ground. Adrenaline still keeps him from registering anything aside from a burning sensation in the fresh wound. Even that is a faint feeling beyond the need to keep moving. He instinctively flips over so he is up right and facing the beast. He quickly walks himself backwards on his hands until he manages to get far enough into the alley to be out of the mutt's reach. The monster paws the space where Dillon was just at a few moments ago. He has to use the building walls to stand up as the fresh wound makes it harder to stand. The beast is still trying to get at Dillon. Dillon decides to risk the noise exposure and pulls out a grenade. He tosses it right in front of the beast who scoops it up in its attempt to grab Dillon. He turn around and limps down the alley as fast as he can manage while counting in his head. *1-1,000. 2-1,000. 3-1,000. 4-1,000. BOOOM!!!* The shockwave sends Dillon flying into some plastic trash cans. He is almost positive that he just heard a few ribs crack as he connects with the waste bins. Once the ringing in his ears clears along with the overall disorientation, he stumbles up onto his feet again. He turns around to find that the mutt is still largely intact. This discovery only adds to frightening mystery of the mutants. Thankfully for him though the front legs and a good chunk of the chest region seems to be sprayed over the surrounding buildings and ground. He cautiously hobbles his way over to the body. Probably not the brightest thing to do in the moment.

Once he is standing directly over it, he whips out his knife and sinks it in the monster's massive head. Ensuring that it is in fact dead. It meets its mark with the ever satisfying and familiar sound that a blade makes when it plunges into a warm body. The resistance of bone and tissue is exponentially greater than if it were a normal person, forcing him to put some of his weight into the blade other than his simple thrust. He manages to relax a bit once he is confident that his prey is dead. Dillon finds it overwhelmingly reassuring to know that even these abominations are unable to survive after getting their chest and half their legs blown all to hell. He decides to pull one of the thing's teeth as a souvenir. He has no good reason for wanting the tooth other than to satiate the kleptomaniac in himself. He pockets the tooth before quickly leaving the alley way the other way in search of secure cover to patch up his wounds. He does not have the need to get rid of the body since he is moving along right away.

Dillon quickly takes off his belt and creates an impromptu tourniquet around where his left femoral artery should be. He is really hoping he remembers anatomy class as well as he thinks he does. Once the belt seems to slow the bleeding to a point that he is satisfied with he continues on. He hobbles along the rears of several houses before the pain in his calf grows so bad that he deems it essential to stop and treat the increasingly bloody avulsions. He practically falls through the sliding back door of the nearest house. If the sounds of his fight hadn't previously alerted every living thing within earshot of his presence, then his thunderous crash through the glass most certainly did. This tumble solicits a low, drawn out groan of pain and misery. He slowly drags himself back upright. Thankfully, his gloves are thick enough to protect his hands from the glass shards. Unfortunately, he is wearing a short sleeve shirt. After a quick once over he realized that he does not have any major cuts or scraps from the crash. His left knee buckles a bit under his weight leaving him with little time to catch himself. He missed the counter completely. A grunt escapes his lips as his forearm scrapped along the corner of the granite countertop. It isn't deep enough to break skin and cause it to bleed but he is likely to have a long red scratch or bruise for at least the rest of the day. He lands on his knees with a thud as they slam into tiled floor with the full force of his weight. He sticks his hands out in front of him in order to catch his upper body. The last thing he needs is to have his face connect with the glass encrusted floor for a second time. The impending agony from the gash on the back of his left calf is gradually making its presence known. Clearly the adrenaline surge from his fight is beginning to subside. That means Dillon has to treat the wound sooner rather than later, hopefully this will help him to refrain from passing out due to the deep-rooted pain. Granted, the blood loss continues to substantially grow with every passing moment so he might just pass out regardless. Fighting through the misery he once again gets back up onto his feet, taking the extra measure of holding onto the countertop.

He quickly scans the kitchen. There are no obvious indications that the previous residents had been drinkers. Or maybe they had, and the place had just been cleaned out of booze when the world shit the bed. Taking this observation into account he figures his best bet is to search under the sink. Using his arms to walk his upper body along the counter, effectively dragging his now cumbersome legs along the floor. He takes extra caution in lowering himself to the ground to avoid any further damage. Once he has positioned himself in front of the cabinets under the sink, he yanks them off somewhat desperately. The old wood creaks in response as the doors flings open. Dillon quickly begins removing the many common things which clutter the dark, damp area. If anyone were to happen across this abandoned old house, they probably would have laughed a little. Dillon looks like a war clad plumber just sending various bottles and containers flying through the air until he finds what he is looking for.

Dillon greedily grabs at the blue capped jug before briefly holding it up in front of him all *Lion King* like. The Pride Rock scene, not the whole your dad getting iced by your uncle and then being in exiled part. He sets the bottle of bleach on the island before standing up. Dillon soaks a nearby hand towel in bleach quickly before wiping off the island. Once he feels content with the semblance of cleanliness that he has restored, he lifts his body up unto the countertop in preparation for the self-aid which will undoubtable be agonizing. He takes the camping Bunsen burner stove and his K-Bar out of his backpack and sets them on the counter next to him. The stove sparks to life with a hiss of propane and the click of the self- ignitor resulting in the *fwoosh* of the small inferno being born. The K-Bar is rapidly bathed in pure bleach and is wiped down with the dish clothe to remove the grime which has built up in the last few weeks. Another rinsing of bleach and the blade is placed on the small camp stove. Dillon has to swing his backpack around so he can fish out one of his extra shirts. He places the bag on the ground to clear up the space around him. The rolled-up shirt is placed in his mouth as a gag to help stifle any screams. After three fast breathes he dumped a generous amount of watered-down bleach over the claw wounds from the mutt. The skin around his face and neck tightened in excruciating pain so that his veins and muscles threatened to burst out of his skin. His scream is largely muffled by the improvised gag. Upon a quick assessment he finds that the four wounds are just far enough up to not affect the Achilles' Tendon. That is about were Dillon's luck ends. Each slice is roughly an inch deep and runs horizontally along his leg for a solid three inches. He can see the bright red muscle fibers in his calf. Unfortunately, this isn't the first time he has been ripped open to the point that he could see the muscles.

Now for the fun part. The knife is now glowing red. He dunks it in the diluted bleach to help clean it off and cool it down a bit so that the blade won't be too hot. Beads of sweat have started to form and flow down his face now. Another three shorts breaths and he uses the blades to cauterize the wound. It takes a while since the knife has to be reheated between each claw mark.

The five minutes it takes him to patch himself up seem like several hours of hell. With the wounds taken care of so they will stop bleeding he removes the belt and returns it to his waist band. Dillon turns the stove off and let that along with the knife cooldown a bit. He bandages the wound in an attempt to further fend off infection. He takes a moment to assess his patch work first aid and is moderately impressed with himself. He had always had a harder time ignoring the pain when it was carried out by his hands. Something about actively thinking about the action and focusing on the area. Or rather that had been his quick conclusion when he had pondered over the observation long ago. This, along with many things, confused Dillon a little. He didn't know if he was weird or if it was something most people could relate to in some aspect. He had learned at an early age that with things like this it was generally a better idea to keep it to himself unless some else brought it up first. Even then it was hit or miss as to whether he would admit to whatever the thought or habit was. Since the knife is still a little warm, he dowses it in bleach one final time before drying it on the rag and sheathing it. The scent of burnt flesh and hair fill the air to create a nauseating aroma.

Now that everything is more or less put away and cleaned up, he decides to get going again. With a swing of his legs he jumps off the island, his left leg slightly gives way for a moment. He manages to steady himself though, so he avoids another face plant. Dillon takes a few steps to see how his leg holds up. It is a dark and disturbing parallel of someone testing a new pair of shoes at the store before they bought them. He thinks he will survive, shrugging he goes to leave. He is almost out the sliding glass door he crashed through originally when something in the corner of the kitchen catches his eye. A simple old broom. The ones that a witch would ride in the old cartoons and shows he used to watch as a kid. His face automatically adopts a crooked half smile. He grabs the handle down by where the straws are connected. He spaces his hands maybe six inches apart before kneeing the thing. The sudden unwarranted act of violence gives way to the loud *CRACK* as the handle snaps in two where he had just attacked it. After the ten or so minutes of whittling the broken end and it is sharpened to a point. He now has a walking stick which doubles as a spear. He ventures down the road several more houses until he finds a safe looking house where he will sleep in for the rest of the day and night in an attempt to try and heal his leg up before continuing on.

The numbers on his watch read out 1100 hours, January 30th, 2030.

Chapter 20

Several miles outside of Aleppo

March 09, 2022

Dillon

"Twenty bucks says it's my turn today." Jacobson whispers to Thompson through the bars separating their stone cells. The cells are cold and hard after being sandblasted into the wall of the cave their captures are using as a base of operations.

"Ha! You don't have the capital to take a bet like that you withered bastard. By my count you're down $350, no, $400. You bet me fifty yesterday that we would have something close to steak for dinner because you told the dumb guard it was our birthday." A worn-down Thompson teases as he starts to laugh despite his prolonged dehydration cause every other word to croak out.

Oh yeah. I guess that did happen, huh?" Jacobson begins giggling as he remembers. "You remember I told Aladdin that even though he can't speak a lick of English?" They both burst out in a strained fits of laughter that do not sound just right since they are constantly on the verge of death by dehydration for the duration of their three and a half stay. They had assigned fucked up names to each of the guards and various other people who came and went. Aladdin was one of the originals guards who had watched over them at the beginning, back when they were clean shaven and at a healthy weight. Neither of them had expected to make it this long nor to be the last ones left, yet here they are.

Today's guard, Sinbad, starts yelling at them in Arabic and banging on the bars of their cells. This is something they are now easily able to understand. **Be quiet!** They immediately hush their cackling, fully aware of the beatings that will follow if they refuse to comply. The momentary distraction from the abysmal hell they have come to reside in perishes. Blinked out in an instant, the fleeting light akin to the lightning bugs one might see flashing on a summer night trying to find a mate. Their sunken faces and emaciated frames assume their prior post. Scarecrow skeletons keeping watch over their sector of hades.

You remember the plan, right?" Thompson whispers to Jacobson. To which he replies "Of Course I do. The damn thing hasn't changed in the last few years except for the number of us." There is a pause where in a single moment they feel an eternity of misery and regret. "How the fuck did we make it to the end when they didn't? Why do we deserve to survive, even in this eternal state of torture? Why are we still alive?" Jacobson breaks down in muffled cries of melancholy. Cries that only Thompson can hear.

"You can't think like that man!" Thompson attempts to comfort both of them with this statement of resolve. "We owe it to our fallen brothers to fight our way through all these endless miles of shit and filth that the world crapped us out into. You owe it to that little kid of yours." Dillon cannot think of anything to say about why he needs to live. He just knows that he deserves all this suffering and hasn't earned the right to die yet. His only regret left in this pit of misery is that his misfortune had dragged down so many good men.

They both sit there in silent suffering. Thompson is trying to count how many scars he has now. He always seemed to lose count around 200. The demons keeping them had sold the men's bodies out to some Victor Frankenstein types that constantly experimented on them. Dobbs and Carmichael had died from the experiments within the first several months. Vega went almost a year after them, Tex and Ramirez went sometime around October. Most of the others had been killed off by the guards getting bored and forcing them to fight to the death. The first time it happened neither one of the men fought and both were beheaded in front of the rest of the prisoners to make a point. Fight if you hope to live. Thompson and Jacobson are all that remain of the 125 men that Thompson helped lead into the meet point that day. They had multiple squads that all got wiped out on the blink of an eye. The remaining men who survived the initial wave tried to rendezvous in a few spots in a futile attempt to ward off the enemy. Their adversaries were better prepared. They had implemented signal jammers so they could not call for help. Their sheer numbers are what lead them to victory over the J-BATS superior fire power. By the time, the last dozen or so were left Thompson had somehow become the highest ranking one. All the officers had been wiped out. Thompson made the call to surrender. Ten of the remaining fifteen listened to his order. The five fighters were soon gunned down along with four of the ten who had thrown down their weapons. Thompson and six of his men were all that was left. The enemy seemed overjoyed to have hostages. Their excitement left the men even more on edge. There had been many other groups to get picked off that day and many more captives to be gained by these cruel bastards.

Sinbad and Jafar have come to take Jacobson away. Jafar only ever shows up if they are being questioned. Jacobson says "Yippee ki yay mother fuckers!" This was the queue they had long agreed on since they all loved those old movies. They open Jacobson's cell and he jumps on them. Thompson bolts up and watches through the joining bars as Jacobson slams Sinbad to the ground and cracking his skull on the ground with a fatal snap. Sinbad is dead the moment he hits the ground thanks to an anchor point for the prisoners' chains which is now embedded into the back of his head. Jafar drives a large blade into Jacobson's side. Thompson wails out at the sight of his last brother in this hell being stabbed. Jacobson spins around and with monkey esk agility he winds his way behind Jafar and uses his handcuffs to strangle the man, twisting his hands to secure the hold. Minutes drag by begrudgingly slow as the life leaves Jafar. Jacobson slumps to the floor once he is sure his target is dead. He fumbles for the keys on Sinbad's waist as more and more blood flows from the newest wound to his side. Once he manages to separate the key ring from the cooling corpses, he crawls his way back up to his feet and slides the keys through the bars to Thompson.

"We did it!" Jacobson softly beams with a grin as he begins to cough up blood. "Go and give them hell for me man." Jacobson gives Thompson one last grin before falling to the ground. Thompson frantically fumbles with the keys to undo his restraints and then unlock his cell all the while begging Jacobson to hold on. He races around the corner and falls to his knees as he tries to put pressure on his friends wound. The injury is to severe regardless of their pour physical condition. It is immediately apparent to Thompson that his last friend shall perish just as all the others before him had. There is nothing left to be done so Thompson holds his friend as he breathes his final breathes.

"You know… I… hated you… the first time… I saw you…right?" Jacobson wheezes with a playful grin. "Who would've thought," He coughs up some blood. Thompson is slowly getting covered in blood. He pays it no mind. "that I would… come to… consider you… my best friend." Jacobson breaks out into another coughing fit. "Tell my son… I fought to… the end."

"Of course, I will, you are such a dumb bastard, now hang in there a bit. You're going to be alright." Thompson attempts to will some of his own life force into his friend.

"I know… just know… I would do… the last few minutes… the same way…because it was…worth it…to give you…a chance." A placid look overcomes his face as he wheezes his final breath. Thompson barely feels the tears flow down his face as he watches the light leave his dear friend's eyes. He lays him down and closes his eyes while taking a moment to clear his and better focus on the task at hand. He switches from man to the beast caged inside. Thompson quickly takes the knife planted in his friend's side and then searches the two guards for any more weapons. Sinbad has an old 20 shot, select fire Stechkin APS. It's an old Soviet pistol from the early 1950's. It fires a 9x18mm bullet. This one is surprisingly clean given its age. Thompson briefly inspects it. The obsessive and frequent maintenance done is apparent to Thompson. The fact that he is holding one at all is astonishing. They had been removed from use and placed into storage by the early 1960's. If Thompson had to guess, some Russians had taken them out of storage and used them to arm soldiers in the middle east during the long cold war that dragged on for another almost four decades after they were removed from service.

Sinbad has around 40 rounds on him. Dillon's luck is starting to look up. Jafar has nothing after stabbing Jacobson with his knife. Dillon walks out of the cell and silently steps down the hallway. There is a dangerous calm which washes over him. He is a predator after all. The tiger freed from the zoo. He has more or less memorized this part of the caves and compounds long ago. He creeps along the left-hand wall. If he takes a left it will take him to the lab where the doctors turned them into monsters. A right takes him to the interrogation room. Considering who was sent to fetch them there would probably be at least three men in the interrogation room. Odds are there isn't anyone in the lab. He slides down the left-hand corridor too the lab. His gamble pays off. It is vacant. He locks the door behind him and instantly searches through all the chemicals looking for anything he might be able to use. He finds several things he can use rather easily. If he had not previously endured the torment from these ghouls he would have questioned if the acids he found were the real deal or not. With those bastard's money was never a problem when it came to chemicals and compounds. These are the real deal. He makes another massive gamble and makes some eyeball measurements to create some impromptu chemical weapons. He grabs a random bone saw just in case he needs more weapons.

Thompson makes his way down the hall leading towards the video room, straight out the lab doors. There are lights flickering through the door crack. Thompson works the door open another few inches so he can get a better view. There are two guards passed out in their desk chairs facing the monitors. Their backs are towards Dillon. He sneaks up behind both of them, locking the door behind him. He puts away the pistol and takes the knife out. He strikes the first man's jugular with viper speed and precision as he clasps a hand over his mouth to keep any possible cries silent. This one grasps his neck momentarily before falling limp to the side. Dillon has killed the second man in a similar fashion before the first one hits the ground.

Dillon locks the second door leading to the guard room so he can look at the cameras and figure out a better plan. He spots 15 men in the guard room, 10 in the room they use for meals, 5 scattered throughout the storage room, 4 in the inquisition room, and another 6 outside the cave as sentries. Dillon makes his way to the door way of the guard room and preps his small chemical bomb. He shakes up the glass beaker of Piranha's solution to make them mixture heat up before tossing it into the room of guards. He slams the door shut and locks it just in time to hear the glass shatter.

He races back to the video room to confirm that he got them. As he had hoped, the hot acid is sent everywhere when the glass shatters causing the men to be splashed with corrosive acid and glass. They are running around screaming in agony as the acid devours their flesh. Dillon makes his way back down to the interrogation room. He peaks around the corner in time to see the four men rush towards the storage room. Dillon rushes up behind them. He stabs one in the neck, instantly ripping the blade back out. Blood splatters all over the others causing them to falter as they realize something has happened behind them. In the same motion he used to remove the blade from the first man's throat he slices the nerves in the back of another man's neck, just around where the C1 and C2 vertebra are supposed to be connected by the Atlantoaxial Joint. The blade is harder to pull out of the man's neck as he collapses to the ground. The man is either paralyzed or dead all together. Dillon brings out the pistol as he drops the blade and fires two shots in the back of both the men's heads. They all hit the ground together.

Dillon charges forward towards the door to their make shift cafeteria. Two men run out just as Dillon gets there. They turn to face Dillon and pause as they prepare to confront him. He keeps sprinting at them just to jump up onto one of the food storage-shelves to the left of them. He quickly ascends to the top and vaults over to the wall separating weapon and food storage near the door to the cafeteria. His grip and strength still aren't what they should be, so he hits the wall a lot harder than intended. Using his hands to help stabilize him a bit he slides down the stone wall, the flesh from his hands and feet is ground away. He lands with a thud, almost completely shattering his fragile legs. His body is pumping so much adrenaline he luckily is incapable of feeling the pain right now otherwise he probably would have passed out due the sheer agony.

The two men are in awe of what this emaciated man just managed to do causing them to hesitate for a few moments too long. Dillon pours two shots into each man. One shot hits center mast and the other luckily managed to hit close enough to graze the left side of his heart, ripping open the pulsating muscle mass and downs the husky man in an instant. The other man receives one shot to the head and one to the throat. The clamorous uproar radiating from the cafeteria brings Dillon back on point. He brandishes a lighter and a Molotov cocktail of pure ethanol alcohol from the lab. The fuse is lit in the time it takes him to breath in and back out, he lobs the bottle into the cafeteria and this time takes a moment to watch as the flames engulf these terrible men. His inner pyro and sadist are both overjoyed watching them run around screaming as they are consumed in a blaze of hatred fueled revenge.

A sinister smile stretches across his weathered face. This jubilation is short lived however as something slams into his back and forces him down to the ground. It is one of the five men that he had seen working in the storage room. Dillon fumbles for something at his belt and removes a syringe which he subtly uncorks before stabbing it into his assailant's thigh, driving down the stopper. The man immediately rolls from on top of Dillon as he wails out in agony as the sulfuric acid burns through his legs, turning everything into a gooey pool of corroded muscles and blood. Dillon rolls away and brings the gun barrel to the man's head as he squeezes the trigger. Even more blood and brain matter splatters over Dillon adding the already extensive compilation of blood and guts painting him a dark crimson.

Dillon staggers up just in time to see two more men come racing down the center aisle between the two main shelves just half a second before they open fire with their assault rifles. Dillon dives for cover at the shelf end nearest the two men he had already attacked. They both now lay in a growing pool of their blood. Bullets continue to rain down and ricochet all around. One grazes his right shoulder, extracting a groan of pain through the adrenaline fueled juggernaut. Dillon soon accepts that he is unable to win this fire fight like this.

Some impulsive thoughts and some crazy ideas lift his ragged body up and give him the strength to push over the shelf he is hiding behind. One of the gunmen is able to dive out of harm, the other doesn't realize what's happening until it is too late. A pallet of food from a higher shelf slides off the shelf as it topples and crushes the second man. The shelf slams down and sends a cloud of dust and debris up, the haze making their vision even worse than it was in the poorly lit compound.

Dillon runs back down the hall leading to the cells under the cover of this smokescreen. The vision only diminishes further as dark smoke seeps forth from the raging inferno consuming the cafeteria and mixes with the dust. He slams into the wall as he rounds the corner, fatigue starting to push through the adrenaline. He drags himself along the wall for several feet, all the blood on him smears across the stone wall. The coarse sediment acts as sandpaper, grinding away more of his skin and worsening his wounds while granting him some new ones at the same time. He stumbles to the ground, chest rising and falling so rapidly he starts to feel light headed. Several minutes have already passed since he started the escape attempt and his body is already beginning to bow under the strain of all the action on his malnourished, withered frame. He can hear shouts slowly gaining on him as his assailants gradually make some headway through the massive mountain of debris that has become engulfed in smoke.

"Get up you bastard!" A voice somewhere inside spurs him on. Dillon lets out a beastly howl as he forces his body upright. He staggers further down the seemingly endless hallway until he burst through the door to the lab and slams into the rusty metal operating table, knocking the wind out of him. As he is doubled over, he notices how much it hurts to breathe now. After reaching his hands up his shirt he realizes that he just broke a rib.

He slowly turns around and bolts the door shut. He needs every last second that he can buy himself. Dillon begins searching through all the various chemicals and compounds in the lab. He hesitates for a moment in front of a mirror as he takes in his appearance for the first time in years. He can see his collar bone poking out of his shirt. Scars cover his body like cracks in worn leather. It is hard for him to decipher were his blood and other people's blood stops and starts. His shirt, the same one that was tight when he set out for that ambush so long ago now looks several sizes too big for the skeleton of a man staring back at him. After this brief once over, he continues searching. He finds more rubbing alcohol, and a hand held blow torch. Once he has taken his shirt off he breaks off part of a broom handle in the corner and bites down with all his might as he begins pouring the alcohol all over to cleanse his wounds then using a red hot scalpel he cauterizes the deep wounds over his body. The veins pop out in his neck as sweat begins coming down his face as he strains against the wood as he screams in agony. He has to take a few breaks whenever he feels pain induced unconsciousness threaten to overtake him.

His breathing has grown progressively more labored during his self-treatment. He throws his shirt back on and resumes his rummaging around until he finds the thing that he wants the most. A tray of syringes filled with adrenaline. Each one had 1mL of adrenaline pre measured out saving him the math. He takes one in his hand and sinks it into his thigh and drives the plunger down. He sends his head back as he feels the rush take hold. That devilish grin spreads across his face again. He rolls his neck and the rest of his joints as he begins to feel back to peak performance. He pockets a few more just in case.

Dillon silently unbolts the door and cracks it open to peak down the hall. The group of men have managed to get through the calamity of the storage room and rush into the cell area to search for him. Dillon creeps out from the lab after the last one disappears around the corner and proceeds to quietly trot down the hall towards them. He leans out from the corner begins unloading his gun into the trio searching for him. They don't have enough to react before they are all gunned down.

Kirtland D. Neal

Dillon heads to the surveillance room again to confirm that he has taken care of all the bastards in here. Some of the screens have gone black now due to camera loss. The one in the cafeteria is out but the hall one just outside of the cafeteria shows that the smoke is still steadily crawling through the cracks in the doorway. The one in the guard room shows the men in there have finally stopped moving after the acid had eaten through them enough. Dillon swipes the boots off of one of the corpses in a chair next to him so he will no longer be bare foot. They are a size or so too small, but he is able to get his feet in them which was all he really needed at the moment. He carefully navigates his way through the acid covered guard room and gets to the other side to the door leading back to the other side of the storage room. This half of the storage room is still intact thanks to the sectioned off walls that mostly separated the two halves. This half is where they stored the weapons while the other half is where the food was kept. He grabs an AK-47, a belt carrying four magazines, and another belt with grenades fixed to it. He isn't entirely sure how many people would be outside and wants to be ready for a small army. He goes ahead and swaps his beat up old pistol for one of the generic old 1911's that is lying in a box of pistols.

He is surprised with what is outside the compound. The small army he had prepared for isn't there. It is instead six men sitting too close to a loud radio. Apparently, none of them had heard anything from inside over the last few minutes. They do not see him coming as he simply lobs a grenade at them and watches as they all get blown to hell.

He proceeds to search the compound for any indication as to when others might show up. There is a letter on one of the desks in the guard room that he finds which seems rather important. From the bit of Arabic that he can still interpret the letter is a kill order. It mentions two men, Jacobson and himself presumably, that are to be executed today. That explains why there were extra people in the interrogation room. They were most likely going to try and question them one last time before putting them down with a bullet in the back of the head outside. There is more in the letter, something about abandoning this compound. The benefactors, whoever they are, seemingly no longer have need of the test subjects and have stopped their funding. The good news is there should not be anyone coming back here. Dillon has more questions than answers though, this whole benefactor's business has him concerned. Pushing that unpleasantness aside he sets to work on trying to get a message out to someone friendly. Over the course of the next hour or so he manages to get an e-mail out to his old command. He falls asleep in the chair a few minutes later.

Chapter 21

January 31, 2030 0700 hours

Tampa, Florida

Dillon

Dillon has slept on and off since the day before trying to rest up enough so that he can still continue on and manage to fight. In spite of his constant insomnia and inability to sleep more than four hours at a time he still manages to catch a good amount of sleep to help speed along his recovery. It is just enough for him to continue on towards Alex.

He is reminded of an old train of thought as he wonders down the deserted streets of the once vibrant city. Each footstep echoes off of the surrounding buildings and shouts back at him. The improvised walking stick adding another layer to the mind numbing echoes following him. A constant shouting voice to remind him of just how alone he is right now. Memories of the days when he wandered from place to place begin flooding back to him. Never allowing anyone to get close. That made them a liability. They made him vulnerable. He had neither the time nor the luxury for such things. He drifted from place to place all while maintaining a decent distance from the rest of the world. Sure, there were some, some who believed they knew the stoic and stern man. They never knew half of what they thought they did. Flashing a cursory light through the darkness and seeing enough damage not to press. None of those people ever seemed to see as far as they wanted. He never let them. Those nomadic days were simple. Easier. The ability to disappear at a moment's notice was a comfort he at the time had very much neglected. Sure, there were unimaginably dark days. Days where all he wanted, all he craved, was to let someone in. Those moments always circled back to the resounding fact that feelings and emotions complicated things, just as personal involvement did. Compassion was a burden he was unable to endure. The concept eventually slipped through his numb hands.

In the face of this cold unfeeling darkness he set up a few measures. His old friends and family. His brothers, mother, father, all his blood family. All of them dead for a long time now. Time had left only a handful of people in his life. Thad, Jill, Sophia, Michael, Ash, Jr., Luke, PB, and Ricci. They had been his nucleus for a long time. The only thing beyond sheer will to hold him together throughout the innumerable tragedies which had plague Dillon much of his life. Over the last year or so he had added Frank to the list. Liz was about as significant to him as a rescue animal you save from the hardships of the outside world. You save it and take care of it until someone more qualified can take over and provide better care.

Since the world rolled over and everything went to hell, he has had to steel himself against the fact that his friends beyond the ones at Pete's are almost definitely dead. This is the only way he can think in order to press on, else his anxiety consumes him. Hope is a weakness he hadn't allowed himself in many long years.

Right now, as he hobbles his injured self towards what he believes is almost inevitable death he craves one thing. That lonesomeness. The icy feeling which hardens his already steely resolve. His gentle humanity scares the ever living shit out of him.

He can do him against anyone in his sleep. But feelings and attachments from people make him incredibly vulnerable. Dillon doubts his current ability to be able to shut out those weaknesses. He is prepared to march to his death. This fact is exemplified by how he no longer feels the throbbing pain in his leg.

Dillon is rapidly approaching the edge of the northeast corner of the Myrtle Hill Memorial Park where 48th street met up with eastbound MLK Jr. boulevard. The roaring calls of unloved engines stop Dillon in his tracks. Dillon speeds up his limped pace towards a nearby mausoleum, the surname adjoined to the crown of the marble structure long since faded beyond obscurity. An initial attempt to use the walking stick to shimmy the lock open results in a broken staff and an unaffected lock.

He grunts with each heave of his rifle as he lands blow after blow upon the lock and chain sealing the safe haven with the butt of his rifle. Beads of sweat flooding over him in the scorching view of the Florida sun. The machinery is nearly deafening when the lock finally gives with a shout and the rust riddled chains rattle to the ground. Dillon shimmies his way into the dusty building and seals the door behind him. He collapses to ground with his bag propping him up against the gate way. Many thunderous heartbeats stampede across his ears before an eternity of hiding passes along with the cacophony of motors clamoring past the cemetery. The rapid rise and fall of his chest struggles to compensate for the thick dust hanging in the air of the seemingly ancient room. The world beyond the stone walls seems to have once again returned to a skewed sense of peace. The grim nature of his surroundings begin to trigger something deep inside of him. Not as deep as it used to be, yet still deep none the less. Dillon is transmuted into something darker. A mental shift as a monster is clawing at the cage. Howling and snarling to be let loose on this miserable world. The bones of the dead glaring at him from all around summoned this beast from the very depths of his personal Hell. The stoic man has been sealed away once more. No way of telling how long this parole will last this time. Only one thing is certain. This devilish reflection of the man is going to make the most of this new found freedom. This is different from the glimpses of daylight this abomination had been granted in recent memory. This was a full-on jail break. Prison guards and Warden locked away instead.

By the time the beast has awoken from his slumber many long hours have passed since Dillon had sealed himself in this monument of death. He jumps up as though all the injuries have disappeared. Dillon spins and kicks the door wide open. The bright light of the full moon leads him out and back towards the fairgrounds.

The next 45 minutes pass by smooth enough until he comes across something unexpected. An image straight out of a nightmare. Another new horror to have been birthed into this newfound hell which gives this battle hardened monster of a man reason to pause. There is a colony of bat-like creatures swarming around the old I-4 overpass. Dillon takes cover around the corner of a nearby building, roughly a football fields distance from the main swarm between him and the overpass. They occasionally land on nearby buildings or vehicles and rummage through the trash searching for food. Dillon only knows they were foraging for food after he witnesses as one of them screeches and tosses out a maggot riddled bag of trash which erupts on the street, sending the colony into a frenzy before flocking to the spot. The carnage lasts only several sickening moments. Even the trash bag and maggots seem to have vanished.

The creatures are maybe four or five feet tall. The biggest amongst them can't be much higher than five foot three inches when standing fully upright. They use the small mangled hands at the end of their wings to walk in a hunched over manner. It almost reminds Dillon of the awkward way gorillas would walk. Similar to the way dinosaur documentaries used to portray the larger pterodactyls would walk when on land. Their furless ash brown hides have a sickly shine in the waning moonlight. Even in the low visibility it is disgustingly apparent that they are completely lacking in eyes. Skin has grown and stretched over where their orbitals may have once been. Their snouts are slightly elongated, and the skin seems to have curled back from the nostrils to make a patchwork maze of cartilage lines. When they open their mouths, the large jagged teeth seem to reach out from their jaws. Ears just as gruesome and twice the size of their skulls protruding from either side of their heads. Their torsos are seemingly thin and frail, the rib cages enlarged from any regular person's. Unlike actual bats, these monsters are much louder and frightening when they make their echoes. A cacophony of overlapping and off pitch screeches and squeals. Deformed after images of the humans they once were, just barely visible beneath the new mutations.

Dillon still has no idea what is causing people to change into these abominations, but he is hoping it is just Mutts and these Dracules. He still isn't great with naming these monsters, but his taxonomy is simple to follow and understand. Needless to say, he will not be assigning them Latin names anytime soon. Just as with the Mutts, he has no idea of how to bring the beast down. Dillon is busy trying to come up with whatever plan has the smallest chance of him getting ripped apart by these creatures when some chunks of concrete fall down next to him. He glances up and much to his dismay one of the smaller Dracules is perched above him sniffing and clicking. His heart almost burst out of his chest at the sight of the beast so close up. His hands begin moving as silently as possible as he reaches for a flash bang in case, he needs to make an abrupt exit. The Dracule soon moves on, doubling back towards its flock.

Dillon, still on edge, peers back around the corner to track its movement. Rifle at the ready. He begins to withdraw back along the main street, eyes never leaving the pack of monsters. He makes it about two buildings before knocking over a pile of trash he did not see. He glances down at the spilled stack of rubbish momentarily before looking back up to see the Dracules coming after, intent to investigate the cause of the noise. Their unholy chorus rebounds off the buildings as the sound grows in volume and intensity. Dillon takes off in as much of a sprint as he can manage. His boots scuff against the aged asphalt, providing the Dracules something new to pursue. Just as beads of sweat turn into full on streams of sweat and his labored breath becomes audible, he can hear them almost upon him. His adrenaline allows him to push through enough pain to run almost normally now.

Despite his frantic searching he is unable to find good building to hide in. He can feel the wind from their flying whipping at his hair now. The cries from the mutated beings is deafening now. It is an absolute assault on his ears, giving him an ever worsening headache. He grabs the flashbang in preparation when he sees it. An old auto repair shop with the main rolling door just barely cracked a few feet. A wicked grin takes hold of his face as his excitement wells into hope. He yanks the pin out as a talon scrapes his left shoulder. He grunts as he powers through his newest injury. He turns to peg one of the Dracules in the middle of the swarm with the flash bang before continuing forward and diving into the garage.

The flash bang goes off just as his tumble comes to a halt. Dillon leaps up to close the door instantly. The wailing creatures scream louder than ever in pure agony as their senses are overloaded. It takes them a few minutes to regain some sense of order before they leave. More confused and hurting than anything else. Dillon decides to stay here until dawn and try and get by while they sleep. Or at least he assumes they need to sleep. He needs them to sleep.

Once the world outside falls silent once again, he sets to work, dealing first with his shoulder. Thankfully, the wound isn't too deep. He rummages around the garage and unfortunately cannot find anything that he can use to sterilize the wound. He has no choice but to roll the dice on this one. He takes out his torch and is about to seal the wound when he realizes that the torch and part of his bag got punctured by the Dracule's talon. The torch is now useless. He screams in frustration as he slams the empty canister against the brick wall. The motion carries from right to left and makes his fresh wound red hot with agony. A pained groan leaves his lips as he angrily mumbles his frustration away. He slams his fist down on the cluttered work bench in front of him sending miscellaneous tools and parts flying.

Think Dammit, think! Dillon begins running through potential fixes in his mind. He begins to rummage through the unkempt garage, desperately searching for anything that might be able to help him. The assortment of tools and parts will be good for assembling various improvised weapons. There are a few flammable chemicals around that may prove useful. Beyond that it is primarily a pile of broken junk. The first aid kit hanging from the wall is empty. He is thoroughly fucked, and not in a good way. Dillon dumps the contents of his bag onto a newly cleared off work bench. Unfortunately, the last of his gauze was used up trying to patch up his legs. Glancing down at his leg it becomes apparent that he needs to change the bandages at some point in the near future. With no other options clearly presenting themselves he starts ripping an extra shirt into ribbons to use as make shift bandages. By the time he gets enough bandages on his shoulder the bulkiness limits his mobility. Unwrapping his leg, he is met with some good news as it show no signs of infection. The bandages reek of sweat and blood. He immediately begins wrapping his leg back up.

After repacking everything back into his ruck he peers through the office blinds and see the faint fingers of dawn reaching across the sky. There is still some blurred movement around the overpass. He still has time to tinker with the random shit he has found. There is enough here to make his half assed plan work. Probably. He makes the decision not to sleep until he takes out the brood of Dracules.

The line-up of cars he has made on top of the overpass make for a beautiful ring of potential destruction. Several buckets of oil and fuel have been used to paint the sides of the overpass. The last two buckets are used to lead his spark of devastation along the sun bleached pavement from his safe vantage point a hundred or so yards north on I-4. He breaks the road flare he scavenged from one the vehicles open. The crimson glow catches his attention as he holds it in front of him. He is completely transfixed in the moment. His eyes adopting that far off sheen they so often do whenever he relives the past. Just as he is about to be swallowed by the phantoms of his misfortunes a roaring machine attacks the air waves, its mechanical shouts splitting the silence in a most offensive way. This sudden jarring is enough to make him drop the flare into the pool of accelerants. The flames race down the path with demonic speed. He realizes the clock has started after it's too late. The noisy disturbance from just moments before immediately forgotten in the urgency of the new situation.

He manages to turn around and step off before the first of the cars explodes into a knurled metallic fire ball. The others follow like dominoes instantly. A concussive blast of burning air and glass rocks Dillon with the force of a pro linebacker propelling him through the air. He connects with a guard rail, his ribs cracking in protest, momentum carries him over and down the hill. He slams into a tree hard enough to knock the wind out of him. The world around him grows a deeper red with each passing second. The world seems to be moving in slow motion for Dillon. The bridge collapses on the brood, their cries sound faint and far away to him. A breathless eternity drags on. He can feel his diaphragm contracting, yet he is still unable to catch his breath. Several agonizing eternities later he is finally able to regain his breath. Everything around him is still very distant. He at last is able to roll himself over and sit up. His hair feels wet. He runs a battered hand through his brown hair. It has gotten longer than he had realized these last few weeks. His hands come back with streaks of blood. It is just enough for concern while not being enough to immediately worry or inhibit him. As Dillon props himself against the tree and drags his weary frame up from the ground. His hearing is still somewhat lacking due to the blast from the explosion. His ears ring like cathedral bells. A feeling he has become all too familiar with over the last few decades.

Dillon starts staggering towards the billowing inferno of rubble to check and make sure his handy work did its intended job. The pitch black smoke rising up darkens an already grim world, soon his world is a hellish collage of a deep red and black. A feverous motion catches his attention in spite of the world closing in around him. A stray Dracule is trying to wiggle free from the wreckage with it's one free wing. Its hideous mouth is snapping open and closed in the same panicked motion of the wing. Dillon is sure that if he could hear it would just be the frantic screams of the trapped monster. Knife in hand he drops a knee on its neck while easily slipping the blade into the base of the skull. The monster spasms momentarily before finally falling still. He slices off the tip of the ear to add to his necklace. The darkness inside him wishes he had managed to kill all of them individually for their trophies. His necklace now has the ear tip and a fang. A blood lust filled grin grows across his face as he realizes he has become a true monster hunter. He is forced to fall back as he begins coughing up a storm. Being this close to the fire is a quick recipe for smoke inhalation. A condition only worsened do the cracked ribs.

His hearing has returned for the most part as he can now hear the fire raging on in front of him. It returns too late as he is struck from behind, dropping to his knees. He must be delirious from the smoke and exhaustion because when he looks up at the figure standing over him. He sees Thad. His shrinking field of vision is soon consumed by the butt of a rifle slamming down across his face, knocking him out.

In a dream like haze he tries to make sense of what he thinks he saw. It is difficult to focus as he is swallowed up by this sea of darkness.

Chapter 22

2nd February 2030

0800 hours

Stinky Pete's Bar

Liz, Frank, Jill, & Sonia

Everyone has been wary since Dillon left the bar a few days ago. The tension hangs in the air, a disorienting fog. Tommy is still barely moving from his room. Mostly because his room stays locked from the outside the majority of the time. Even though he promises to be on their side everyone knows he said that in front of Dillon and that was after a week or so of torture. None of them are entirely certain what Dillon had done to Tommy, but they are sure that they didn't envy him at all. Jill, Sonia, and Frank have no pity on him. They had all known him prior to the world losing its mind. Even on Infection best of days he had never been a great person. Jill knew that his hands had been bloody long before the rule book had been tossed out the window.

Liz has offered to tend to him since she was a nurse in her past life. Their encounters the first few days she was taking care of him were uncomfortably silent for her. That was back when Dillon had just let Tommy back in from the garage. She has been slowly taking to him more and more. He still does not respond to her, so she is forced to mostly tell him stories. She spends a lot of time talking about her sister Tabitha.

"Tabi was always the smartest one of the family and yet she was always kind of embarrassed about it. I never understood it. Truth is I was always looking up to her even though she was younger." Liz prattles on as she removes Tommy's old bandages. "She had gotten this really secretive job that she wasn't able to tell us about. Our mom was very skeptical at first until Tabi started getting paid and began sending money back to help the family. She seemed immensely proud of the work she was doing. Funny enough I only came here to see her. I waited and never heard from her. She said if that had happened that she was most likely tied up with work and not worry so I…."

"Shut the fuck up!" Tommy growls as he finally breaks his long lasting silence. "No one gives a fuck about your dumb cunt of a sister or the rest of your family. Odds are they are all dead now. Just learn to accept that fact and move on, You worthless cow!"

By now Tommy's raised voice has drawn the attention of Jill as she walks down the hallway. Liz rushes out in tears as she begins to think about the possibility of her family being dead. She is so distraught as she runs away that she doesn't notice that she bumps into Jill. Jill walks into the room to confront Tommy.

"I don't know what you said to that poor woman, but I swear to whatever excuse there still is for a god that I am going to make sure that you regret it." Jill's rage bubbles over more and more with each condemning word. She has now crossed the small room and is standing over the bandaged figure with his back to her. Her rant continues on for what seems like an eternity. She pauses in the midst of her berating and reaches down to roll him over so she can look him in the eyes while she yells at him. "Are you even listening to me?"

She barely lays her hand on him when he strikes. He uses the old bandages and quickly wraps them around her neck and squeezes. Her hands desperately reach for her throat as she falls forward and Tommy jumps on her back.

He has been planning this since he told Dillon where to go. There are enough monsters and security between here and Alex that Dillon should either be dead or easy enough for Alex or even a severely injured Tommy to finish off. He just had to wait until he was healed up enough that he could fight and had an opportunity to catch one of these morons off guard. The fact that it was the one person who didn't know him made it easier. She would have a somewhat fresh perspective of him and would eventually be taken off guard when he lashed out like he did. He is rather impressed with himself in regard to how well that part has worked out. He honestly never expected the grown woman to cry and race out of the room. Jill being the strongest person here just makes her all that much better of a target. With her out of the way he would have a much easier time escaping.

Jill is beginning to shake as she is strangled. Tommy is all but guaranteed to succeed now that she is about to die. He thinks he hears something behind him then something hits him in the head, and everything goes dark.

Sonia and Jill are both breathing heavily. Jill is still trying to catch her breath as the black spots slowly drift away. Sonia is shaking with all the adrenaline racing through her system. She is surprisingly okay with what she has done. No, that isn't it. There is something more concerning. Or rather something which should have concerned her more than it actually does. She is excited.

Some small part of her enjoys what she has just done. Some unseen embers have just been fanned into a small fire. It is more than revenge for what he had put them through. He deserved it completely, but that isn't why she enjoyed it. She can't remember a time when she had felt more powerful or in control. Her face remains a stoic mask concealing the swell of triumphant jubilance growing just beneath the surface.

Once Jill has caught her breath and can process what has happened, she becomes overtaken by a sea of emotion. A new found appreciation for life, which now a days is saying a lot. She is grateful that her daughter had saved her, but that gratitude is in direct conflict with the realization that her sweet baby girl has just killed someone. Jill has to admit that while Tommy did have it coming, she had never imagined it would be her princess who would do it. The cold steely blade is glaring back at the two women telling the story of what has happened. The blood flowing forth from the wound in the back of Tommy's head confirms that he is in fact dead. Jill is unable to think of anything to say to her daughter, so she just walks out of the small room. The scent of iron trails after her as she staggers down the hall in shock. Crimson footprints make a bread trail back to the crime scene. Jill locks herself in her room upstairs as she struggles to come to terms with the newfound reality that her child is a killer as well as how closely she was to dying. Any desire or thought of cleaning up is completely nonexistent to the distraught woman.

Sonia walks down the hall and stops in front an old wooden door. A royal blue base with metallic gold roses and vines are painted across an aged door. The once pristine finish had long ago begun chipping away, bit by bit. A pale, grime covered reflection of its former glory. She raises a still bloodied hand in front of her face and absent mindedly raps her knuckles against the faded door. There is a brief pause which stretches on forever in the morose atmosphere of the current situation. The door slowly creaks open to reveal Frank in workout clothes. Beads of sweat incredibly apparent as it flows down in rivulets and his chest rises and falls. Evidence of him sticking to the regiment that Dillon laid out for him. The exhausted smile on his face is suddenly replaced with a concerned look of abject horror as he begins to process the blood riddle girl standing before him. His mouth hangs open in astonishment.

"Long story short, Tommy tried to kill my mom in what I'm assuming was escape attempt. I heard a noise and came running. I saw it and used the knife I had on my belt and plunged it in the back of his head. Mom went upstairs and seems to still be in shock over it all. I need you to help me to deal with the body." Sonia's explanation is uncharacteristically cold and callused.

Her demeanor is oddly devoid of feeling. It is almost reminiscent of Dillon. This frigidness accompanied with the news of Tommy's sudden death disturbs Frank. She doesn't wait for him to respond before she turns and walks back to towards the body. After a brief hesitation Frank follows her. The silhouette leading him seems like a stranger to him. The figure disappears around the corner as she ducks into the room. A putrid aroma of blood hits Frank the instant he sees the growing lake of blood flowing out of the room. The metallic scent is almost palpable. If Frank had anything in his stomach, he is sure he would have thrown up.

Chapter 23

Tampa, Florida

2nd February 2030,

0900 hours

Dillon

For a long time after waking Dillon is unable to open his eyes. The hair on the back of his head feels wet and his body hurts all over. A passing pothole painfully lets him know that he is in some sort of vehicle. A metallic droning noise confirms his suspicions. He tries to raise his hands to his face. Pain once again shoots through him. Thick, cold metallic restrains keep his arms behind his back. The awkward posturing launches him in the side of the vehicle as the driver makes a turn. His shoulder is ground into the wall forcing him to cry out as the still fresh wound burns white hot with irritation. With the final painful jostling he realizes that he can in fact open his eyes, it is just pitch black. How the fuck did he get here?

"Good, you're finally awake." A familiar voice says as the hood is ripped off his head. Dillon's head whips around. A disoriented animal trying to take in its new surroundings. The van is still dark, but dimly lit enough for Dillon to make out three figures sitting across from him. The front two seats of the van are occupied by more mysterious figures. The questions begin flooded his mind as he attempts to satiate his internal need for answers and real information. Dillon's gaze re-centers on the large figure in the middle of the trio facing him. He seems to be leaning forward in an engaging manner. It is only bright enough for Dillon to make out the silhouettes of his enigmatic captures. Even still, something about this great, brooding figure seems familiar to Dillon. The notion is nagging away at him, there is something he is forgetting. What is it? The silence between him and his captors is more deafening than the rattling of the engine. It takes him several agonizingly long minutes to retrace the last few memories he had. The bridge…the last Dracule, and then….

"Thad?" Dillon croaks out, the smoke damage is more audible than he had expected. The single word sends him into a minor coughing fit. His attentive audience waits in muted anticipation. Once his coughing subsides, he restates his question. A deep sigh fills the entirety of the van in response to his question. There seems to be a heavy sadness and hopelessness contained in that sigh. The following silence is all the answer that he needed. Now he is forced to muster all the remaining emotion he has and fill it into a single word. With a handful of letters strung together he will use the last of his humanity that has yet to be locked away.

"Why?" There is a crushing tenderness to the word that hadn't come out of Dillon since before his family had died. Just the after image of the gentle man he had been made Thad's eye's well with tears. The giant of man is thankful for the lightless void of the van as he swiftly wipes away the tears. He hadn't heard his friend sound like this in many years. This unexpected flow of nostalgia and emotions just break Thad's heart even more considering what he is about to tell his old friend. The explanation seems impossible to make his friend understand. It is truly a shitty situation in which there is no good way to explain it.

"It's complicated D. I can't really say too much right now. That's the Boss's job. We were just sent to investigate a loud explosion near the Colony last night, which I now know must have been you taunting with those Leather Wings."

"That's the shit name you bastards gave them?" Dillon scoffs, any emotion or kindness is absent from his voice once again. The battle hardened man and his demonic companions have returned. The kind and gentle man who was rattled to the surface by the reappearance of his old friend is once again laid to rest. "Guess who ever this dipshit boss of yours is too fucking stupid…" He is interrupted by an unseen hand back handing him. The size of the blow lets him know that it isn't Thad who hits him. He spits out the bit of blood festering in his mouth before carrying on. "… to even attempt a decent name for those impish li'l fuckers. I've been calling them Dracules, like Dracula." Dillon beams defiantly. Another hand strikes him across the face. Just as with the first one the sound of the impact momentarily fills the van. Thad does nothing to chastise the unknown assailant. He may be bound and betrayed, but Dillon will be damned if he isn't about to taunt and goat these bastards to the point that he can escape.

"Believe me Dillon, I wish I didn't have to do this. There were orders to bring you in if anyone found you. There are people who seem to know what you are capable of and what happened to you. Things I'm not allowed to know and things only a few people ever knew, or so I had thought." Thad tries to explain, his tone holds a slight hint of remorse and…bitterness. Not enough to win Dillon over after this V.I.P. treatment though.

"What about Jill and Sonia? What will they think?" Dillon rebuttals to this poor excuse for an explanation. He can hear the big man shift awkwardly as he utters those names. Something is off here. Dillon feels even more on edge. The tension in the air now is like electricity running across his skin.

"Well, I had been taking people out of town to my cousin's place just past Plant City where I knew they would be safe on the farm. It was mostly one's or two's, people we had known before the shit hit the fan. Jill and Sonia had insisted on staying at the bar. Plus, Ernie wouldn't leave, and I didn't have the heart to be the one to make him sober up to this fresh hell." *Fair point about Ernie.* Dillon thinks to himself as he shrugs in the darkness. "Then about the end of the first month or so of this shit I get a call on the radio from a larger group that needed my help. Some old neighbors from back before I built the bar. The group was too big to fit into my car so after I met up with them, we all walked out there. We were about half way there when we seemed to have gotten ambushed by a pack of those giant dog monsters."

"Mutts." Dillon offers his name for them assuming it would be an improvement on whatever they had imagined.

"Well these Mutts, as you call them, were different from the others I had seen previously. They seemed to be older than any of them should have been. That wasn't the weirdest part of it either. They were in chains. They tore through the group in an instant, thought I was next. When suddenly a whistle from beyond them halted them. They behaved like feral hunting dogs. It was even more terrifying than seeing them run wild." Dillon is now leaning forward as much as his restraints and the bumpy ride would allow him without falling to much more. "Just then, Alex came out from behind the Mutts. He gave me two options. Work for him or me and my girls would get ripped apart."

"So, you *are* working for a fucking dumbass!" Dillon cackles for a second before he is once again struck across the face. This time it is a boot that cracks him. His laughter carries on for another few moments in defiance before resuming his silence as he eagerly awaits the completion of the story. "What about your family?"

"I tried to leave the compound once shortly after arriving and I was caught and tortured for three days straight." He makes a gesture to scars hidden in the darkness of the van.

"He only tortured you for three days? What did he not have the stomach for anything longer?" Any pity the former prisoner of war may have had has long since dried up. He is again kicked. His question is left unanswered.

"He brought me the bodies of my girls on the third day and made me realize I had nothing left worth leaving for. He broke me Dillon." The large man begins to sob a little before being cut off.

"Are you fucking kidding me? There's no way you're this much of a cowardly dumb fuck as to have believed that and then just rolled over and become his whipping boy. First of all, the girls are alive and well! *I* saved them from Tommy, who was sent by Alex! I have been training and protecting *your* fucking family while we kept searching for you! Come to find out you've been turned into Alex's little bitch doing his bidding and believing every dumb thing he tries blowing up your ass like smoke up a chimney!" This time the fist that hits him is absolutely Thad's. Dillon moves his lower jaw in a circular motion to try and loosen it up a bit after the last hit. His nose is definitely bleeding now. Probably broken, again. The van comes to a screeching halt before Thad is able to respond. The double doors at the back of the van are flung open and Dillon is momentarily blinded by the bright light of mid-morning.

Apocalypse Virus: Initial Infection

About a dozen guns are immediately trained on him. He almost feels honored by the warm welcome. Alex stands in the center of the gunmen. The halo of rifles reminds Dillon of some old promo poster for one of those warlord movies. He decides it is best not to giggle too loudly on this one.

"It's my pleasure and honor to welcome you to my humble little community D-man. I can see they have been warming you up a bit in the cold of the winter." Alex greets him in his ever thick Puerto Rican accent. A Cheshire grin is spread across his face. He motions him closer. A request answered by the men on either side of Thad who *help* Dillon get out of the van. Thad is carrying Dillon's gear. Alex brings Dillon in for a cartel like embrace.

"Hello my old friend. I hope you know how I plan to return your *hospitality* when I get loose." Dillon growls into Alex's ear. The words are twisted with malice and feel like venom in Alex's ears. No one else hears his greeting but the two of them. Alex tries not to let it show how much these words startle him, but Dillon can tell. A sinister grin now adorns the shackled man's face. He rears his head back and rams it forward as hard as he can manage. Alex shouts out and staggers back, blood trickling down from his the freshly broken nose. He wipes his nose on his sleeve as Dillon is slammed face down into the ground by several men behind him.

"Now we've both been *warmed up.* Come get me when you're ready for some alone time." Dillon boasts as he is lifted up and escorted through the compound. He keeps repeating the same greeting to each group he passes, "Thank you, I know how excited you all must be to have me here. I'll be here all week." This rewards him with many confused looks and the occasional elbow to the ribs. The large man writhes and twist in demonic glee as he is roughly ushered forward. The group of degenerates hanging around the old cracker country definitely fit the description Tommy had given Dillon. All the old buildings have been tagged, multiple balconies and porches have been smashed. A charred patch of earth is all that remained of one of the buildings. Trash and broken bottles litter the area. Some of the trees have people hanging from them as vultures do drive-byes slowly picking the flesh off the bodies. Most of them are naked. Some have various slurs and insults carved into the skin. Screams from in between two of the buildings catch Dillon's attention as several men are forcing themselves on some nameless woman. The majority of the occupants pause their activities to gaze and sneer at Dillon as he is led to a make shift prison cell area in the big building at the edge of cracker country near the pond and old power of steam building.

Someone had cleared out the majority of the building's interior and welded various scraps of metal together to make some rusty, apocalyptic looking prison. *The world did basically end a several weeks ago.* Dillon mentally shrugs to himself at this revelation. The thugs escorting Dillon walk him to the most desolate looking cell at the far end of the building. He is rushed past the other cells too fast for Dillon to get a good look at the other captives, but he is able to tell that most of them are overcrowded. Various cries and scream form a deafening echo in the small building. He is shoved through the open door of the only vacant cell left. As he stumbles forward a boot catches him in the back of the knee sending him falling forward.

The men kick him several more times before slamming the cell door shut. The cell is extremely bleak even in the middle of the day. Dillon's mind begins to play the greatest hits of all his worst memories from those few years in captivity. He begins shaking and sweating as he further unravels into the episode. Every painful moment flares across his nerves all at once. The long buried faces of his unit run through his mind. The only pause from the endless loop of guilt are the periodic glimpses of the tests and torture the scientist made him endure so long ago. The old soldier's flashback carries on for an eternity. Eventually he throws up and passes out next to the pile of vomit.

The next week or so blows past Dillon in the blink of an eye with a flurry of PTSD episodes and brief periods of light torture from what Dillon thinks of as subpar amateur torture. None of it is anywhere near as bad as what he had previously suffered nor what he had done to Tommy. Minor league stuff like electroshock, being crushed by immense weights, being submerged in hypothermic baths of ice, being beaten on like a punching bag, strangling, being pulled in either direction by chains attached to his wrists and ankles. He also endures being used as a human ashtray. There is more in the following days and intermissions as well. Despite how agonizing this hellish treatment is, Dillon still feels oddly more comfortable in the constant state of mental and physical torment than he had in a long time. With each hit, cut, flashback, and every crack of the cattle whip or zap of the car battery they seemed to gradually melt away all the tension that had been building in his muscles. Carving away at what remained of his soul. His eyes grow even more devoid of expression. The spark in those steely blue eyes goes as dark as a black hole. He devolves ever further into the numb monster he had kept caged for so long. The beast inside, devouring more and more of the man known as Dillon. Each passing moment it becomes less and less likely that he will ever be able to return to who he was.

This was never Alex's desire. He drops in twice a day to check on the man he had long respected and feared. The same man who had once been like a teacher and older brother to Alex. Each visit leaves Alex more unsteady than the last. Regardless of his uneasiness, they press on. Alex needs Dillon to join them even if he won't explain why to everyone else. Thad hadn't been able to stomach the sight of his old friend in this condition and hadn't seen him since the first day. The fifth or sixth day his flashbacks stop all together. The same day he stops reacting to the physical stimulus. A cold, unfeeling corpse with a pulse and foggy thoughts. On the seventh day he begins to howl with laughter, growing ever louder with each subsequent blow. A devious and maniacal grin splits his face open from ear. By middle of the eighth day no one is willing to touch him. The final few shreds of humanity he had desperately clung to for all these years has finally been stripped all the way away. Potentially forever. This was never Alex's intention. How could he have known the darkness inside of his old mentor was this bottomless, this infinite? The bad inside Dillon resembles outer space that way.

Not one living soul had ever seen him like this. He had killed all of them who had. All, except for those damn trench coats when he managed to break out. Would this be the same? He aches with desire at the thought of ripping every last one of them apart. Alex seems to sense this blood lust and decides after the ninth day that it is time for the next stage. Dillon is given some extra days to rest and hopefully return to his old self.

Chapter 24

Stinky Pete's Bar, Tampa

09 February 2030

1200 hours

Dillon

Jill is pouring herself another drink as she waits on the others to return. She is unable to remember what drink she is on now. It has become common practice for her to drink all day in the last week as she refuses to confront how close she came to dying as well as her daughter killing someone in order to save her. She is putting the bottle away when Frank walk in from one of the rooms. They make eye contact and he gives her a half defeated look that says *"Really? You're drunk this early again?"*

She scrunches her face in disgruntlement as she responds to his judgmental glare. "Fuck off! Yous can't drink alls day without starting first ding in da morning." The impairment is only emphasized by her stumbling back to the other side of the bar to retake her seat at the bar. Her elbow slams along the bar top and knocks off an old photo album she had been looking over for the better part of the morning. She slowly bends about half way over to reach for by the time Frank has crossed the distance between them to pick the book up for her. She had already shown him the entire book three times in the last week. He places it on the bar next to her without saying a word. He continues out to the garage just as silently to grab some ammo so he can go stand lookout on the roof until the girls get back. If today is going to be like the last week had been, then Jill would most likely be passed out at the bar in another hour or so for her afternoon nap.

Frank still isn't sure what to make of the new found alcoholism that Jill seems to cling to so desperately. He is trying not to judge her too much after everything that had happened with Tommy but, she has been extremely selfish and not even thinking about the rest of the group. Frank is scanning the surrounding area while thinking about how things have been the last week and a half since Dillon had left them. For the most part he felt they have been doing fairly well all things considered. Aside from Tommy and then Jill's drinking, everything seemed to be going along great. They were slowly checking surrounding buildings for not only any sign of Thad, but they are also systematically scavenging as much useful materials as they can find. They have already extended their search radius five blocks. Yesterday Frank had gone out with Sonia searching and they come across a half-eaten corpse of some sort of massive monster. They both shuddered to think of what this thing may have been when it was alive or even worse, what could have killed the massive creature. The skeleton was roughly eight feet long and both of them could have fit in its rib cage. Liz went sheet white when they told her. They made the decision not to tell Jill until she finally decided to sober up. She was slowly becoming a problem that none of them wanted to confront just yet but is clearly becoming an issue. Liz shares Franks mindset on understanding Jill and just letting her work through it on her own time. Sonia had tried to snap her mom out of it the morning after Tommy died. The screaming match which ensued only seemed to make her worse off. Each passing day since she seemed to worsen, slipping further into a semi-permanent drunken stupor.

Sonia seems to have changed in Frank's eyes since she killed Tommy. She seems more excited whenever they run into some sort of trouble. An uneasy hunger or blood lust seems to have steadily consumed her since her first kill. There was a small group of thugs that had chased Frank and Liz back a few days before. Sonia was overjoyed and giddy with excitement as she began to mow them down from the lookout perch on top of Stinky Pete's. Once they had gotten through the door, double over and out of breath she was super energized and ready to head out without them to search for more of the thugs to fight. She had seemingly shifted from the tough yet kind girl next door into this modern day Red Sonja type of warrior woman. Frank is torn between arousal and terror. Frank had to spend several minutes arguing and pleading with her to stay because both him and Liz needed a breather. Eventually she reluctantly agreed to his request.

The beeping of his watch brings him back from his deep thoughts. He finally realizes the date. Tomorrow is his 21st birthday. He had completely forgotten about his would-be plans he had made so long ago with his friends. He is going to miss his mom's homemade cake and cooking for the first birthday ever. He was never much of homesick person. Yet, somehow this sudden realization that for the first time in as long as he can remember he will not be eating his mother's cooking on his birthday. He never will again. A deep pang of sadness over takes the empty heavy spot in the pit of his stomach. Up until now he hadn't given too much thought to anything other than surviving and keeping things going. He is now unable to think about anything other than him never seeing his mom again. He is overwhelmed with all the things he so often took for granted. That warm sense of safety and peace he felt with all of her hugs. How they could spend hours taking on the phone each week about all the small trivial things that were happening to them in their day to day life. The way she smelled. He never knew what it was called but his mom had always used the same fragrances which he come to associate with the smell of home and protection. Silent tears begin cascading down his face as the loss of his mom and everything that meant hit him like a freight train. He had never had an easy life growing up, but his mom had often been his entire world even if he was only now realizing it. Before long he is crouched over balling into the palms of his hands. In his distress he does not hear the gentle tap and rattle of long, pointed legs going across a nearby rooftop. The screams from the street are similarly lost on him.

Liz and Sonia set out from Pete's under the early cover of the ever reaching fingers of crimson signaling the impending dawn. Their search route today is taking them farther away than they had been so far. They manage to find a few untouched bottles of liquor and not much else. The sun soon bares down on them with renewed intensity of the impending spring just a few brief weeks away. The girls quickly agree that they have searched enough for the day and begin to make their way back. They do the usual way of taking a new route back so they can increase their search radius. They are a few blocks away when they begin to notice a nightmarish landscape unfold around them. It is a scene taken right of the pages of a Lovecraft or King novel. Several buildings they had passed a few days before are now undistinguishable amidst a patchwork mountain of spider webs. Some of the thread is almost invisible, others are as thick as a telephone pole. As they press on, the street grows dark as it morphs into an ever darkening tunnel sprawling out before them. The other side a small fleck of light beckoning them forward with false hope.

After sharing a brief glance of uncertainty, they cautiously press forward through the webbed world of nightmares. Several impossibly large bodies are spun up randomly throughout the tunnel of thread covered terrors. About a dozen or so seem too bizarrely shaped for them to be human. The girls keep themselves from imagining the horrors beneath the spun webs. Before long they are walking shoulder to shoulder, hesitant step for hesitant step. Regardless of how amazing and powerful Sonia had come to feel in the last week this environment reduced her to a scared girl again.

Liz feels an odd sense of comfort as she walks with Sonia walking so close to her. Liz knows she should have weird feelings about the strange comfort and safety she feels from being near a girl half her age. If she was being completely honest with herself, it was mostly just having someone right next to her. Sure, who it was helped. The emotional connection that had been built over their brief time together helped to reinforce these feelings of security. She would have never realized this aversion to loneliness without all the doom and gloom. The comfort of this interaction was as shocking to her as the strength of her relationship with Sonia and the rest of the group. These new bonds made Liz confront her sudden alienation from her cozy world. The very real possibility that her sister had died in some swamp not too many hours' drive from where she is. She's shaken from her tail spin of melancholy reflection as she bumps into the back of Sonia, who has stopped in her tracks. Liz peeks her head around Sonia' shoulder.

"Why did you…?" Her question freezes in her throat as she sees what is causing Sonia's mouth to hang open. It's Stinky Pete's. They can clearly make out Frank, doubled over crying. This isn't what had frozen the girls. It was the monstrous creature casually coming up behind him. It is almost definitely responsible for the hellscape they had just travelled through.

It has eight long, jagged legs. The tips are scaled in a way that gives them a similar look to serrated blades. The jagged legs are an alternating pattern of auburn and gold. The abdomen is a massive oval shape, maybe six feet long by four feet wide. They can't tell how thick it is from their angle. The abdomen is a sunset orangish-yellow with a flecked pattern of grays and blacks rippling over it. The ass-end of it had a pair of spike like appendages. The front end gives way to a mostly human looking torso. Only instead of skin there are more fuzzy scales, this is a macabre pattern of grays and blacks. What were once arms are now multi-jointed palps. They are all black and shiny. On the shoulders of the monster is an even more gruesome composite of human and spider features. The hair had thinned out drastically and a handful of small spikes have grown out like a crown. The original eyes have enlarged to roughly four times their original size and a second pair half the size of the main ones have grown outward and upward. The nose have flattened into almost indistinguishable slits. The mouth has spread almost cheek bone to cheek bone and is now adorned with two large fangs which seem to snap back and forth as the beast draws closer to Frank.

The girls begin shouting to get his attention. He does not notice them as the monster got ever nearer. Their legs begin driving them forward, each step faster than the last. The hot, stale air sears the skin of their throats yet still this pain is barely registering as the blood and adrenaline pump away. A desperate surge of energy in a small hope to save their friend. Soon the pavement beneath their feet gives way to the concrete floors of the bar which quickly become creaky wooden stairs and then the weathered rooftop. The spider rears back and spits a massive glob of white goo at Frank, hitting him square in the back. The impact knocks him over as the glob seems to explode and envelop him. In an instant his wriggling body is encased in the sticky substance. Liz is frozen in horror after witnessing all of this. Sonia, on the other hand is not frozen. She begins unleashing a barrage of bullets on the monster. An ear splitting shriek comes from the beast as it is assaulted, causing Liz to quiver and shake herself out of the fear induced paralysis. In half a breath she too is firing away on the thing. In seconds it begins to withdraw towards the edge of the roof. A massive predator being bombarded by annoying, stinging pests. In spite of its reaction, there appears to be no real damage even after several minutes of firing upon it and gradually driving it ever closer to the edge. The monster, clearly annoyed and losing interest, turns and retreats beyond the rooftop's edge.

"Liz! Go cut Frank loose and drag his dumb ass inside! Now!" Sonia screams over the sound of gunfire. Liz turns and lunges for her friend, clearing the table between them effortlessly. Frank has stopped moving inside his silky prison. The already rising wave of panic and fear solidifies into ice stopped in her veins when she sees his limp cocoon. The knife on her hip is frantically ripped out of the holster, ripping the snap locked hilt strap in the process. She eagerly begins cutting away the casing as carefully as she can in order to avoid slicing Frank. "He isn't breathing!" the fear in her voice cuts through the noise around her more than her volume. "Sonia, Frank isn't fucking breathing!" Any remaining color has now left her cheeks.

"For fuck's sake!" Sonia exclaims, "Just get him the FUCK INSIDE Liz! We can deal with the rest when we don't have a god damn monster right there."

The young girl really is taking after her uncle more and more each day as the world around them spirals further into madness. Liz struggles to drag the young man inside. His slim frame is very misleading, his weight proving to be substantially more than she originally wagered. Sonia creeps a little closer to the edge as she reloads. She is trying to peer over the edge and find out how far the monster has gone. She does not have to go too close as she sees the thing scuttling away over the network of webs to a spot several buildings away. Not wanting to miss an opportunity to finish this now she seamlessly lobs two grenades at it. The explosions rock the building as the swaths of webbing a few buildings over explode into a fiery impact zone, the cries of the beast very clearly different than before. Sonia is hopeful that even if this doesn't kill the monster, it will at least be very hurt. She turns back and helps Liz drag Frank the last few feet inside. The trio collapse on the ground as the door to spider hell shuts behind them.

Frank still isn't breathing. Sonia checks for a pulse. It is slow, but still there. Liz is still a whirlwind of emotions and freaking out. It is vastly different when the person you are supposed to be giving medical attention is someone you know rather than a stranger. "Go down stairs and see if we still have the machine." Sonia orders Liz, more so to get her out of the way than anything else. She starts doing compressions like she was taught by Dillon forever ago before he left.

"Come on Frank, come on." She urges, "You can do it, come back to us. Please!" she is pleading now. Three rounds later and she's beginning to fear the worst. Tears start flowing forth from her eyes at the thought of losing him. She isn't ready to lose him, she hasn't even…. His sudden coughing and wheezing halt her attempts to save him. She is overjoyed that he is breathing again. Slowly he starts to come to again, eyelids fluttering open to find a weeping Sonia leaning over him. He is unable to remember what happened. Why isn't he on the roof anymore? Before he can articulate his question, the jubilant young woman grabs him by the face and pulls him in for an impassioned kiss. After the initial shock of the action he relaxes before returning her embrace. Liz is making her way up the stairs at that moment.

"Hey, I—" She stops talking immediately after seeing the two interlocked. Satisfied with Frank being alive she turns and walks off with a thin grin displaying her approval. The two have more than earned the right to do what they wanted. She is simply glad that they are okay.

Chapter 25

Florida

30 December, 2029

Tabitha

After more than a week of exhaustively trying to decipher the stolen information Tabitha is giving up hope that she can ever do this. She has also been forced to stay on the move in order to avoid being found by her former employer. She still isn't entirely sure if they had noticed their copied data or not yet, but she doesn't want to risk it just yet. The backseat of her car is overflowing with empty coffee cups and cans of red bull. She has had maybe a few hours of sleep since she had left with the information. The sleep deprivation and constant crying have taken the young, robust woman and drastically aged her in just a week.

Knowing now that she is ill-equipped to tackle this problem herself, she is starting to prepare to outsource the issue to someone who can handle the task. And more importantly someone who will hopefully do the right thing with the information. The better part of the last 30 hours have been spent scouring message boards on activist and terrorist pages. Tabitha even takes a brief dive into the dark web around lunch. She has a fairly good feeling she knows who she is going to send the information to. There is a hacktivist who had gained notoriety across the web for various accomplishments he had done over the last decade. One of the biggest was exposing and bankrupting the Rothschild's and all their interest which had been manipulating the world for the majority of the last century. He also wiped all student loan debts across all of America. Twice over. The hacker went by the alias of MR.INHUMAN55. Somewhere on the dark web there was a list of addresses to mail things to for the clients and potential collaborators use whenever something required little to no digital footprint.

Luckily for Tabitha, one such drop box was located maybe half a day's drive away. She quickly plots a route without security cameras before packing up her stuff and getting back on the road. The lengthy road trip proves a pleasant break from the usual hours spent toiling over the computer. She does run into a slight issue about an hour or so into the trip as she begins nodding off behind the wheel, forcing her to pull off onto some side road. Being paranoid and careful she hides the car.

Tabitha is awoken by the startling crackle of lightning in the distance. Her breathing is frantic as she searches around her. Ensuring the demons of her mind are simply that. Nightmares. A glance at the clock on the dashboard reveals that six hours have passed since she pulled off the highway. *Dammit!* She mentally berates herself for being this careless. Tabitha angrily wipes the sweat from her brow as the key turns over in the ignition. The engine purrs to life simultaneously while the metal frame whips back onto the road and barrels down the highway towards a final destination.

Many agonizingly slow and dull hours later and Tabitha is pulling up to a pier. A seemingly abandoned old building greets her with a smaller companion to the left of it. A series of docks spread out behind it, fingers reaching ever deeper into the ocean. A NO TRESSPASSING sign hangs on every door and window of the two forgotten structures. Rusty, dust covered metal chairs and tables litter the space between buildings. Fancier, wooden table and chairs are the broken skeletons in the tombs of glass and concrete. The clock on the dash reads 11:23 pm. Another thirty or so minutes and it will be the New Year. A full moon and fireworks illuminate her search around the building, desperately looking for any sign that she is in the right place. The large sign which had once been mounted above the entrance now lays on the floor in front of a boarded up set of double doors. The grimy sign has seven abused letters adorned upon it. *Circles.* Tabitha is preparing to move on from her search when she sees a symbol carved crudely into to edge of the sign. It was a 3-*D K with a crown hanging atop the upper left line. A* trade mark symbol of Mr.Inhuman. A small arrow is etched alongside it pointing around the corner, towards the second building. She slowly walks over to the dilapidated ruins of a bar where she finds the same symbol painted on one of the few remaining taps. Tabitha makes her way around the back side of the bar and starts searching for more symbols. After ten minutes she returns her attention to the Yuengling tap with the symbol painted on it. She pulls the tap back as if to pour a drink when a small camera slowly emerges from the spigot before flashing a picture of her. The flash leaves her panicked, just before she bolts the camera retracts and a note drops out of the spigot next to it. She freezes in her tracks as her curiosity and desperation begin to drive her, she picks up the note and reads it.

I am neither hope nor salvation

I salvage what was lost and hidden

Both good and evil, I have condemned

Kirtland D. Neal
I burn the world down, never scorching myself

Water can never burn

Freedom and Justice fly highest at SEA

If my assistance is what you desire

Turn you back on the East

Avoid being blinded by the west

Find me on the fingers

You must know me too find me

The cryptic poem ends. She sits for many long minutes mulling it over. She launches up with excitement as she believes she has solved it. Making her way over to the piers she begins searching. She is unable to find the symbol from before, so she starts thinking about everything she has learned about him. Replaying it like a bad soundtrack in her head as she continues her search. Then it's there, staring her in the face. A large sail boat with an odd Latin name is bobbing up and down as the waves washed past it. The symbol isn't on the boat though. It is on the wooden beam sticking up from the pier right next to center of the hull. She hesitantly walks forward and begins searching the post, trying to hold back the small surges of hope and excitement that have begun welling up inside of her. Initially no one would even think anything was special about the post beyond the small bit of vandalism adorning the shore side of it. Tabitha runs her hands over it lightly so as to avoid getting splinters while also trying to feel for any abnormalities. On the opposite side of the post from the marking is a small indentation which has a little bit of give. Before she even stopped to think about the consequences, she presses the indented button. With a small, barely audible hiss and click the top raises up half an inch. She unscrews it as much as it will give and there is cavity within the center of the post. An unseen speaker whispers a message in a robotic voice.

Apocalypse Virus: Initial Infection

"You have found me! Congratulations! If you truly require my aid leave your mystery inside. Your response will be in the news before too long. Breathe easy wayward soul for your plight has been heard and you will be helped in due time. This shall be your only visit for this will not work twice for you. Be safe, stay hidden and be on your way."

It sounds more like a message out of those old fantasy video games. She quickly withdraws the packet of information which includes a hard drive of all the still encrypted information she had failed to crack the code on. The package hits the bottom of the hollowed out chamber and after a brief pause the weight of the item seems to have triggered some mechanism as it sinks a little further and the lid closes itself. The indent is now flush with the rest of the post. True to the voice recording she is unable to reopen the hidden compartment. She feels a massive weight lift up from her shoulders. She no longer has to worry about the truth dying with her. Walking back to her car, fireworks exploding overhead, she begins to cry tears of joy and relief. In a way the excitement of the rest of the world is her own celebration. This burden is no longer hers alone. She almost sinks into the seat and melts as she enters her car. Tabitha pulls away and will never again think of the decaying pier side restaurant.

About a fifteen-minute drive she checks herself into a real hotel. The first real bed she has slept in over the last week or so. She messages her sister and tells her that she has already paid for her plane ticket and to get on the plane first thing in the morning. She calls her to make sure she sees the message in time. It is hard to reassure her older sister that everything will be alright and that everything will be explained in person when she gets here. The selling point is "I just need my sister to be here right now." With this emotional sucker punch her sister submits and agrees to come. With her sister on board she hangs up the phone and goes to sleep. She is fairly confident that she will not actually get to see her sister, but hopefully this will lead her sister to more answers than Tabitha currently has. Content and at ease for the first time in many long weeks she lays down on the bed and falls into a deep sleep.

After several long hours of blissful slumber, she is awoken by a mysterious figure entering the hotel room. She silently sits up in the bed and waits for the shadowy person to creep ever closer before she flicks on the bed side light. The intruder is physically startled. Unsurprisingly enough to her, she knows the-would-be assailant. It is her former co-worker and STS shadow conspirator, Ricco.

"Hello old friend." She calmly greets him, showing no signs of fear or confusion as he had expected. "You don't seem surprise to see me. Why?" His face is contorted with concern.

"I was hiding around the corner when you, Mr. Mackenzie and that raven man were talking about me after the break in. I've known for months now that I was under suspicion. My only question is why now?" She is trying to bait him one last time before he undoubtedly kills her.

"When the security guards were routinely drug tested your *friend's* test came back with rather abnormal results. Your absence was also noted and cause for concern, but the two things coinciding with one another raised more and more alarms. We went back through all the badge logs and altered footage you so expertly edited."

"Thanks." She says behind a fake smile.

"We couldn't exactly tell what all had been taken, we almost dismissed the event all together until we had discovered that a vial of your serum was missing along with a secret one called **Darksied.** At that point it was easy to pinpoint who had taken them since you were the only employee with any irregular behavior. I will give you credit Tabi, you sure can hide well when you want too. We always seemed to be one step behind you." He phrases his old friend as he makes his way across the small room.

"Thanks, so is this the part where you kill me or are you going to talk me to death?" She flatly taunts him.

"One more question first. Where are the vials?" He says as he brandishes his weapon. It is a FNX 45 Tactical with a Trijicon RMR sight on top. He smoothly attaches a SilencerCo Osprey 45 silencer on it as he awaits a response.

"I can't seem to remember where I placed it." She confidently says with a proud and defiant grin.
"That's a shame Tabitha. Guess I'll just have to say it got destroyed in termination. Goodbye Tabitha." He sounds almost sad to have to take out his old friend. Yet, regardless of any emotional hesitancy the pistol is still raised.

"Goodbye Ricco." She says as a single tear falls from her eye. The muffle cough of the silencer goes off several times as he puts two in the chest and one in the head. Ricco disassembles the gun and hides it once more before walking over and closing her eyes. He places a gloved hand on her forehead before planting a kiss over the glove. An odd sign of respect for the women he just murdered. The gloved hand is to avoid any DNA traces.

After a fruitless search of the room he turns off the light and leaves, placing the do not disturb sign on the door handle as he walks out. He pays for the room in cash for three more days claiming his girlfriend and he are having a special weekend. A search of the car proves just as useless. Either way none of it will matter in a few days. "It is done sir, what's next?" He reports into his phone. He falls silent for a long time as he receives his next assignment. "Yes sir. It will be done." He clicks his phone off. He is grateful that for once he won't have to commit to the arduous task of cleaning up since none of it would matter soon. With the job done and the body slowly cooling he sneaks out and makes his way to his final assignment.

Over the next few days, he flies almost non-stop, leaving behind clothes and traces of himself at each airport in his assigned region. Numerous other agents carry out similar missions across the globe in order to usher in a new era.

About the Author

Born in Pensacola, Florida, Kirtland Dean Neal grew up as the oldest of four boys in a military household. Tampa would become where he calls home after his family moved there when he Ten years old. He left Tampa at eighteen when he joined the Air Force. This new venture would take him back to Northwest Florida before whisking him away to the beautiful Okinawa, Japan.

He has always had a profound love of reading and storytelling. Some of the first things he ever wrote were little poems to give his Mom on her birthday and Mother's Day. Even as a young boy, he had a dream of one day publishing a book. He used to think it would be a book of poems until he was able to begin crafting detailed stories. His profound love of learning, nature, the outdoors, science, and art have shaped him to not only the writer he is but also the man he is today. He now actively pursues a career as both an actor and author, wanting to create art that has the power to connect to people.

If you have made it this far then I hope that you enjoyed the book. That is all I could ever ask for.

If you have any questions, feel free to message me. I welcome any fan art you may have of the monsters. I would love to see how my mutants look in your mind.

Kirtland D. Neal
Main Instagram page @Mr.Inhuman55
Art Instagram @inhuman_art55
E-Mail kirtlandneal.writing@gmail.com

9 781737 787204